I0626701

Surrendering Stinkin' Thinkin' Series
Book 3

You're Brilliant

Hannah Arduini & Julie Arduini

Book 3

Surrendering Stinkin' Thinkin'
Series

You're Brilliant

Hannah Arduini

Julie Arduini

ISBN: 978-1-7336876-3-8

Copyright © 2020 Hannah Arduini, Julie Arduini

All rights reserved. No part of this publication may be reproduced or transmitted in any form or by means without written permission from Surrendered Scribe Media.

This book is a work of fiction. Names, characters, places, and incidents are either products of the authors' imagination or used as fiction. Any similarity to actual people and/or events is purely coincidental.

Scripture quotations are taken from the Holy Bible, New Living Translation, copyright ©1996, 2004, 2007, 2013, 2015 by Tyndale House Foundation. Used by permission of Tyndale House Publishers, Inc., Carol Stream, Illinois 60188. All rights reserved.

Cover created by Surrendered Scribe Media, photos courtesy Shutterstock.com, Pixabay.com

Published by Surrendered Scribe Media, Youngstown, Ohio, 44514

Julie Arduini offers a free download of her contemporary romances, Entrusted and Entangled for those who subscribe to her twice-a-month newsletter.

She includes encouragement and book suggestions as well as writing updates and promotions that benefit you.

https://mailchi.mp/321e32f02e17/juliearduininewsletter
or visit the right sidebar of
http://juliearduini.com

Surrendering Stinkin' Thinkin' Series

You're Beautiful: Brilliant Things Happen when a group of girls and their mentors discover they're beautiful.

Hayley Atkinson withdraws from her friends and new opportunities with the new mentoring group, Linked, after she is told a lie that she believes is true about herself.

Sabrina Wayson is a mentor in Linked who feels she can't help encourage girls because she's struggling as much as they are. Can they surrender the lies and find freedom?

YOU'RE AMAZING: Beautiful things happen when a group of girls and their mentors discover they're worthy.

Jazmin's a natural at dance until a series of changes make her wonder if she should even keep up with her favorite hobby.

Lena's a mom with young children overwhelmed with her schedule when a woman remarks that what Lena does isn't even important. Both Jazmin and Lena belong to Linked, a mentoring ministry where all ages encourage each other and build friendships.

Can these two surrender the lies they are believing and realize they are amazing?

YOU'RE BRILLIANT: Amazing things happen when a group of high school students and women discover they are more than competent.

Bethany's not excited to start high school in a new community where she doesn't know anyone. She quickly befriends KJ, a popular sophomore, and it looks like the transition will go well until Bethany discovers KJ's boyfriend is a bully. With a strong sense of justice, Bethany challenges Brent Sullivan, and he's determined to make her suffer.

Cheri takes on an additional job in a school to help pay for Sabrina's wedding. It's a different atmosphere than at the church where she feels more comfortable as the pastor's wife and mentor with the Linked ministry. After several mishaps, Cheri feels like she's found an assignment where she can make a difference until a teacher belittles her work.

Can Bethany and Cheri resist the lies about their competency and hold on to the fact they're brilliant?

A Message for Readers:

This series was inspired by Hannah after a tough transition to junior high. Instead of giving up and becoming bitter, Hannah decided to take the lessons she learned and create a series for girls her age. Julie (Hannah's mom,) has a passion for mentoring. As she listened to Hannah create characters, Julie realized there was a message in Hannah's work for women, too.

Each book in the Surrendering Stinkin' Thinkin' Series uses the theme of letting go of a lie the characters believed. There will be two key characters in each book. One, a student, and the other, a woman out of school. It's our desire to see girls of all ages (even grandmas!) read these books and find freedom and hope in them.

Hannah created the storyline, character names and traits, plot points, and conflict. She had the vision for the cover, and directed Julie in the design. Julie wrote out Hannah's vision and managed the writing and publishing process, staying true to Hannah's creation. *You're Brilliant* is a work of fiction, but a message of hope for you.

Dedication:

To girls of all ages who have been told they can't do anything right, or feel like failures for whatever reason, you are brilliant!

CHAPTER ONE

Bethany Tuttle

One glimpse at the sprawling Boardman Valley High School campus and my throat starts to close. It's my first time here and what a fortress. It's twice the size of my old school. So many windows. Multiple parking lots. Three athletic fields. There's even an attached brick circular amphitheater to house the enormous drama and musical talent the Youngstown suburb is known for. What am I doing here? Oh, right. My parents moved and this is the closest school district. Where I know no one.

Students fresh off the bus travel to the main entrance. I'm trapped in the middle of the swarm, moving with the wave of peers, my anxiety escalating with each step. Even if I wanted to yell for help, I wouldn't be heard over the buzz of first day chit chat filling the lobby.

A boy with a head full of curls and wearing a *Saturday Night Live* shirt bumps into my side. "Hey, tourist. If you don't know where you're going, step to the side."

"Sorry. Did my fanny pack give me away?" I smile at my attempt at humor, but no one chuckles or even looks in my direction. There's so much movement. "Say, are we students or cattle?" My voice rises above the fray, but I sound like a squeaky kid.

"Keep mooo---ving funny girl." The tall blonde surrounded by three girls mimicking her every move, throws her head back and laughs. Her minions follow her lead and they're giggling with her.

I'm not as agile as my friend Jazmin, but I've got stealth working for me. With a few ducks and weaves, I exit the throng of people and slam against the wall next to the office.

A slim, tall girl with shiny, straight brown hair is about to approach the receptionist when she looks my way and tilts her head. "Are you Bethany Tuttle?"

I raise my eyebrows. How does she know my name?

She gestures me forward. "C'mon. I'm KJ Curry. I'm the student council rep the vice-principal lassoed into keeping you corralled." Her expression is sober for about a second before she breaks into a chuckle.

KJ heard my cattle joke. And thank God, she thinks I'm funny.

She gestures toward the office door, and I nod and push the lever, walking into a reception area that feels more like a prison entry. A bulky security guard with a black mustache and no smile stands to the right of the sign-in area.

KJ saunters in like she has the keys to the kingdom. "Hey, Mrs. Erickson. How was your summer?"

A woman sitting front and center behind a long counter and a few clipboards smiles, her gray curls bounce as she reaches for a stack of papers. In the middle of those loose ringlets is a splash or purple. "Full of fun with the grandkids, thanks for asking. My daughter also appreciates your babysitting skills. You saved her more than once during the break." The woman with a lot more warmth than anything I experienced in the hall directs her smile toward me. "Bethany? I have your schedule and emergency forms here for you."

I look to KJ, so overwhelmed by the earlier chaos it's as if I've lost my speech. She nods, and like her puppet, I reach for the paperwork.

Mrs. Erickson's either clueless I'm nervous or ignores my shaking hands. "You and KJ have almost the same schedule. She'll help you out. First days are overwhelming."

Finally, I find my voice, probably somewhere next to my courage. "Thanks. This place is huge."

KJ moves her backpack to her other shoulder. "You'll get used to it in no time. Promise." She turns toward Mrs. Erickson with a wave. "Glad you had a good summer. See you soon." The door opens, a ridiculously tall guy wearing Under Armour gear strides through, giving us the chance to exit. As we do, the boy high-fives KJ. Girl appears to be popular.

I peek at my schedule and notice homeroom is on the second floor, and so is my locker.

KJ uses her height to glance at my paper. "Your locker is right near the stairs. That will come in handy. You have three minutes between classes. Teachers are pretty easy about being late the first week. Be careful after that." She seamlessly maneuvers into the crowd, navigating us toward the stairs. At least half a dozen greetings come her way.

"You seem pretty popular."

She shrugs. "I'm active in a few things. Plus, my boyfriend is kind of known. He's a junior and plays football."

I want to slink back down the stairs and call my parents. Even if there was a guy interested in dating me, my dad made it clear I'd be sixteen before the discussion would even be allowed. KJ has definitely got the life. "Wow. How did you meet?"

We arrive at my locker and I toss the medical papers in before slamming the narrow door. Most lockers are decorated in some way, designating cheerleaders, football players, soccer members, drama team, or even student council.

KJ passes a few rows before we land at her locker. The front has student council and soccer symbols on display. "Pep rally. I was assigned to help him find the right balloon arch to walk through." She giggles, revealing wide brown eyes. "I know, really romantic right?"

You're Brilliant

How do I reply to that? It's not exactly a date movie I'd pitch to Netflix, but hey, she sure is living a life I don't have. I decide to move on to a different topic. "So, are you stuck with me all day?"

KJ rolls her eyes and delivers a light punch to my upper arm. "No way am I stuck. I signed up to do this. Trust me, Bethany, this place isn't that bad."

I resist the urge to rub my arm and look at my schedule again. Homeroom is three doors down and the bell's about to ring. "I'll take your word for it."

Before she can reply, a guy looking like something out of a cartoon with rusty hair and a broad chest crashes into the lockers. KJ doesn't jump or flinch. The guy glowers at both of us before closing the gap between us and making our triangle more of a couple and an odd Bethany out. "KJ, is your phone on?"

It's time for homeroom, so I take his question as my cue to exit and offer a limp wave before slinking away. I don't hear her reply, but his seems to bounce off the walls. "I'm sick and tired of telling you KJ, when I text, I expect a reply. Lots of girls wish I'd text them. Could you take the time to actually answer your boyfriend next time?"

Prince Charming stalks off in a huff, and I turn to check on KJ. Our eyes connect, but she looks away and swipes at her cheek. Looks like I'm not the student having the worst day at Boardman Valley.

CHAPTER TWO

Cheri Wayson

This job is to help Sabrina pay for the wedding. I repeat the words every step I take as I walk away from my parked car to the Youngstown middle school entrance where my niece/adopted daughter works. Three months ago I didn't know I'd transition from pastor's wife and ministry leader to public school employee. But for Sabrina? Chet and I would move mountains for that girl.

Students who come up to my chest or higher rush by, pushing through the main doors with typical first day energy. I filter through the pack and enter the office, praying my red maxi dress and black leggings are appropriate attire for the job.

"Mom? There you are. Over here." Sabrina's voice rises above the chatter and we lock gazes. She waves me over to the staff mailboxes, arms open wide, offering a hug that I need as much as I desire another cup of coffee.

"Sabrina, thank goodness. I wasn't sure what I was supposed to do."

Her smile could light the block. "I can't stay, but I wanted to make sure you found your way. Mr. Tucker's waiting for you." She pointed to the door attached to the office with a nameplate bearing the principal's name.

I loosen the grip on my purse so I can feel my fingers again and brush my moist palms against my dress. "Were you this nervous on your first day?"

Sabrina's laughter fills the room. "You and Dad do remember waking up to the sounds of my throwing up, right?"

Her ability to laugh at herself helps calm my nerves. She waves and dashes off to her eighth-grade classroom. I meander to the door and softly knock three times.

"Come in." The baritone voice sounds friendly enough. I turn the knob and find the principal on the other side of the room near another door. "I was just about to greet students in the hall. Cheri Wayson, right? Care to join me?" Although he carries an intimidating presence with his impressive height, shiny bald head, and dark beard, his smile disarms my nerves.

My inch-high boot heels make it challenging to catch up to the six foot or so man, but I arrive at his side as he steps into the hallway. "Yes, the assistant principal interviewed me and told me to ask for you when I arrive. I'm not exactly sure what my duties are."

Mr. Tucker glances my way for a second before offering a high-five to a petite girl who looked to be in the sixth grade. He returns his focus to me. "We have several areas that need assistance, but I'm still hiring. How about for now we try you out in different places and see where you fit best?"

I greet a few students who traipse by before replying. "Sounds good. Where do you want me first?"

Mr. Tucker smoothed out his tie and gestured toward the cafeteria. "Let's begin with lunchroom duty. If you can make it here, you can work anywhere."

Memories from Sabrina's lunchtimes as a student come to mind. Food fights, spills, pushing in line, but it is all worth it to help these kids become kinder, friendlier people and to earn the money to help my sweet girl marry the man of her dreams, Charlie Shell.

18

In two hours' time, the cafeteria manager, Marge, and her sister, Carmella, teach me the fast track of middle school lunch time. With hair net in place and fashionable boots that are rubbing against my heels, I descend on the beverage station ready to quench thirst and offer smiles.

The first troops to arrive are the hungry and nervous sixth-graders. Like me, it's their first adventure in the cafeteria. One-half races to the kitchen and the other half runs toward the tables. Two teachers stand in the middle and start directing traffic. *My goodness, this is busier than when the church has potluck dinners.*

Once kids go through the food line, they arrive at my counter. "Good morning, how's the first day going?" My attention is on the first few, but no one looks at me. They're grabbing cups, milk cartons, and straws.

"Carter, get out of the way. I want the orange juice."

"Wait your turn. I'm getting lemonade."

"Nevaeh, throw me a chocolate milk."

I reach for the dairy and hand one to the girl with beautiful ebony braids. "Let's not toss anything."

No one hears, and to save time, one boy already starting to grow facial hair picks up a milk and throws it down the line to his friend. Then someone else thinks juggling cups is funny before he hands them out to friends.

My voice quivers as I try to find authority in my tone. "Children, please don't do that. We want to keep everything clean."

Still, no one hears. One of the milk cartons flies above my head and when I catch it, I squeeze too hard, puncturing it. "Watch out!"

You're Brilliant

It's too late. Milk splatters in a girl's hair and down her front. She shrieks and takes her cup full of pink liquid and throws it back in the direction the dairy came from. This is getting out of control, fast. "Please stop! Someone's going to get hurt." I barely finish my plea when a sixth grader with glasses heads toward our area reaching for a cup when he slides on the pink milk mixture.

Mr. Tucker stops mid-stride, spins a U-turn, and rushes my way.

He reaches out and catches glasses boy and grabs him by the shirt before the kid lands on his backside. The boy straightens, his eyes wide, and steps over the mess. My boss holds both hands up and all beverage traffic stops. "Ladies and gentlemen, this is not how sixth graders behave. Ever. Am I clear?"

Of course, now they all choose to listen.

In two minutes, Mr. Tucker calls maintenance and men with mops take over the area. He moves teachers closer to my station for traffic control. Then he approaches me. "I was in the military before college."

I look around to find something I can do that would help me appear useful. There's a cloth near the juice station, so I bunch it up and wipe the counter. "I apologize. It got out of hand so fast."

He nods and strokes his bearded chin. "Take a breath. Seventh grade should be better."

I lift the cloth and notice a cluster of activity. "Is that them?"

Mr. Tucker walks toward the chaos like a soldier sent to face-off against the enemy. He turns toward me. "You'll be fine. Use your authority and draw boundaries. I'll check in at the end of the day."

Hours later, when I finally exit the building, my heels are so raw I'm carrying my boots to the car. I limp down the steps praying the tears don't start until I'm behind the steering wheel. Mr. Tucker's last words were, "The cafeteria isn't for everyone." I smell like expired milk and orange juice.

Chet's inside the garage waiting for me with a bouquet of roses. I leave the boots in the car as I trudge toward him.

He hands the flowers over as he hugs me, planting a kiss in my milk-splattered hair. "How's my hard-working wife?"

I can't even try to smile I'm so tired. I hold the flowers in one hand and brush at the corner of my eye to get rid of any tell-tale tears. "I'm a failure."

You're Brilliant

CHAPTER THREE

Bethany

My parents complain that adulting is hard, but facing a cafeteria where everyone scatters toward their peers in hopes of approval and a seat at the table, torture. Middle school was easy. We all knew each other, and I had Jazmin and Hayley always ready with a chair and a chocolate pudding to share. Those days are over. I scan the room and don't see any familiar faces, but at least there's an empty table in the far corner.

My tray hovers over the table ready to land when a bunch of plates drop with a thud. I look up to find three built guys wearing football lettermen jackets and sneers. "We're sitting here."

I lay my stuff on the table and quickly sit. "My tray was hovering before you got here."

The three sit with such force I brace myself to go airborne. One opens his milk and takes a swig without a straw before resting his arms on the table and staring me down. "You're a freshman. We aren't. Find somewhere else to sit."

His voice I recognize. It's KJ's boyfriend, and there's no way I'm backing down from a bully, even a handsome one with steel-blue eyes.

"Here's the deal. I'm not just a freshman, I'm new. The proper thing would be to let me have a seat. We can even share. You can talk about your sports stuff and I'll eat my corndog."

The beefy guy on the left with no neck squints as he examines me. "Hey, you're the girl from this morning." He elbows KJ's boyfriend. "She called us all cattle. Then Brindi made cow noises at her. It was hilarious."

You're Brilliant

While they laugh it up, I decide to make use of having a table and chair and start eating. No-Neck stops his cow noises once he realizes I'm still there. "Hey. Time for you to go."

I lay the corndog stick down and pick up string cheese, slowly peeling away. The jock on the right looks to KJ's boyfriend for guidance, and the ringleader doesn't disappoint.

"You think you're pretty funny sitting there ignoring us."

"You're the one with the goofy look on your face." Just thinking of how he talked to KJ fuels my sass—ignites his anger.

He pounds the table and No-Neck's milk carton moves. "Little girl, leave or we'll help you."

Still working on my string cheese, I pick up my milk container, open it as if I have the rest of the day, and in one fluid motion, pour the liquid across their laps. With an angry holler, the three stand, veins popping out of their foreheads, faces turning a dark crimson. Their rapid movement draws a crowd, including a teacher who joins us.

"What's going on here? Sully, you aren't harassing freshmen again, are you?"

Sully. So that's what we call KJ's boyfriend.

Sully looks down at his wet pants and glares at me, pointing. "She dumped milk on us!"

The slim teacher with sweat beads on his lip crosses his arms against his chest and faces me. "Is that true?"

I shrug, stuffing my hands in my jeans jacket. "They weren't welcoming me."

The man sighs. "Well, I'll tell you who is welcoming. All of you to the office. Mr. Burke will deal with it."

24

Heading to the principal's office isn't how I pictured my first day. But at least my pants are dry. The teacher escorts us, probably to make sure I don't get stuffed in a locker.

I sit in the waiting area while the boys go to the rest room to wipe down. The door marked "Principal" opens, and a man shorter than my grandpa with just as much gray hair walks up to me, lips pursed. "Were you part of the lunchroom disturbance?"

The guys enter, and I clearly see wet splotches across the front of their pants. *Don't laugh.* "If you mean that I refused to bow down to their threats, then yes."

No-Neck points to his wet spot in case no one noticed. "Mr. Burke, she did this to us."

The principal pinches the bridge of his nose. "Okay, all of you inside my office. Looks like I get to spend my afternoon calling your parents."

Parents. I didn't think through this freshman-standing-up-against-the-bullies thing.

I hope when I get off the bus that my parents are still at work and forget all about their chat with Mr. Burke. The tired administrator sent me back to class before I could hear the conversation. As I linger at the mailbox, leafing through ads and political cards, my text notification dings. I peek at the screen and it's one of my BFF's, Hayley.

How was the first day of school 😊

I stuff the mail under my phone and offer a quick reply. *Visited the Principal's office* 😧

You're Brilliant

Wow. Do your parents know?

Now that I've reached the door, I slurp in a breath and shoot one last reply. Depending on how they react, it could be my last.

Entering house now.

Praying. LMK.

Prayer is something I should have activated back in the cafeteria. When my dad's glare is the first thing I make contact with, I wish I'd never stepped foot in the new school.

"Bethany Ann Tuttle, have a seat."

The mail crinkles as I clench my palm. "Dad, I can explain."

He holds up his hand and I know not to speak. I snap my jaw shut and sit across from him at the dining room table, the phone and mail set off to the side. His brown eyes, always so kind, look empty and sad. "Explain to me how you landed in the principal's office the first day of high school."

"The short version is I sassed some upperclassmen jocks and dumped milk in their laps."

Dad's face reveals nothing, and that's worse than if he was full of fury. "Give me the long version."

With a sigh, I think back to my terrible day, starting with the morning. The one bright spot was meeting KJ. "There was a student council rep who helped me find my locker and spent some time with me. Her name's KJ and she's super sweet. When I started to go to homeroom, her boyfriend came up to her and was a jerk to her." I note the slight tilt of his head. "For real, Dad. He was controlling. Scary. And him and his buddies tried to bully me out of a lunch table I was already standing at."

26

"Okay, go on."

"I kept thinking of how this Sully guy treated KJ and how they were trying to intimidate me. I got mad. And that's how you got the phone call. How much trouble am I in?"

He rubs his eyes in a way that reminds me of Mr. Burke. "You have consequences to face at school. Two weeks detention. Because the event involved bullying, you will serve your detention after school right away. The gentlemen in question will have a month of detention once you finish. They're also on probation with football."

Ugh. They still get to be in the gridiron spotlight. "How about with you and Mom?"

Dad stands and gestures for me to follow suit, and he walks over and gives me a rare hug. "Bethany, we knew there had to be a story for you to act that way. I'll talk with your mother later, but you've always had a sense of justice, and in this case, I understand. It means you need to be careful. Those boys may try to retaliate."

"I'm more worried for KJ than me."

He releases the embrace. "Her job may be to assist you as a freshman, but it sounds like God is using you to remind her of her worth."

"I'm supposed to break them up?"

Dad shakes his head. "No. There's a lot to this situation that needs adult supervision. But it sounds as though KJ doubts herself if she allows herself to be treated so cruelly by this boy. I'm glad you see his behavior as wrong. At the same time, don't take justice into your own hands again."

I glance at the floor, wishing I could turn back time. "I'm sorry I disappointed you."

You're Brilliant

Thankfully, when Mom comes home and they talk after dinner, the two decide not to punish me. I go upstairs so I can text Jazmin and Hayley with a lighter heart. I'm in the hallway when a text comes through.

Got your number from the student council paperwork they gave me. What happened at lunch? My BF says you got him in trouble. We need to talk. KJ.

CHAPTER FOUR

Cheri

Seems as if most of the Greater Youngstown residents chose Mugs for their Saturday coffee destination, just as I have for our Linked planning meeting. Frustrating. I scan the area for an empty table and smile when I see sweet Lena Calloway waving from one in the corner.

I greet the mother with a hug. "How did you manage to get here so early?"

Lena, looking refreshed after a recent anniversary trip, gestures to the other empty seats. "No kids. Bryce is home with them. It's easy to manage my time when I only have to worry about myself." She wraps her hand around her oversized red cup. "Thanks for asking me to help plan the next Linked meeting. Is Sabrina coming?"

I pull my credit card from my wallet. "She'll be a little late. Charlie's close to presenting his doctorate work to the board, so he's practicing and Sabrina's giving feedback. I'll be right back."

Once the barista places my tea on the counter, I return to our table and open my planner. "It's so refreshing to be working on the mentoring ministry. This week with school starting, I've been wrapped up in my job and it's so new. Working with you, Sabrina, and the girls at church is my peaceful place."

Lena sips her drink. "Why is it you're working at the school?"

My mind flashes back to Sabrina in tears. Her biological parents are addicted and unable to provide for any of her needs. Her fiancé facing a move across the country for a teaching job once he graduates in December. Sabrina spending more of her teaching paycheck on her students than her wedding. "Chet and I prayed about it and we wanted to help pay for the wedding. I'm working at the school and he's picked up some extra income as an Uber driver."

You're Brilliant

Lena sighs. "Bryce and I were on our own for our wedding. It sure can be a stressful time. How's your job going?"

My shoulders drop as if invisible cement blocks rest on them as I flash back to on my first week serving in a public middle school. "I'd love to say it's been a smooth transition and I'm a natural. The reality is the school had a lot of renovations over the summer, staff transitions and upheaval. I was a last-minute hire by the assistant principal, but the principal wasn't sure which area to place me because there are so many places where I could serve."

"It doesn't sound very organized."

That's an understatement. "You're right. I tried the cafeteria and that was mass chaos. I ended the week in the library and the eighth graders snuck in inappropriate books and displayed them on the new book shelf. I didn't know, so the sixth graders tried to check them out."

Lena shook her head. "Oh, Cheri. That sounds terrible."

The pit in my stomach grows as I wish the weekend could last. But as Sabrina glides into the café, a wide smile accompanied by a romantic glow on her face, I know working at the school is the right thing for me. And planning Linked meetings with Lena and Sabrina is a blessing.

Sabrina needs no caffeine for our time together. Her excitement wraps around our little corner and helps take the burdens off my shoulders. She hugs us both before sitting. "Sorry I'm late. Charlie's still working on his thesis. I can't believe how close he is to his doctorate."

Lena moves her chair to give Sabrina room. "And your wedding. And moving. There's so much going on!"

Sabrina squeezes her fists together and releases a small squeal. "It's crazy. But God is so good. Who knew my future husband lived right in the same development where I grew up?" She turns to me. "But enough about me. Let's talk about the girls. I want them to have the best year with Linked."

Inside my planner is a folder where I've clipped pictures of the regulars, the girls that attend nearly every month. Hayley Atkinson, the freshman who reaches out the most to Sabrina when she's feeling unsure about herself, especially her appearance. Jazmin West darts to the refreshments first, but with her metabolism from dance, she maintains a healthy outlook and is entertaining. Bethany Tuttle's always ready to offer a joke, but she recently moved and is adjusting to a new school. Jade Green's been a challenge with her moods, but Sabrina feels she's a Linked success. Emily Santos is our new transplant from Akron, another dancer, but she has to work harder at it than Jazmin. The pictures remind me to pray. "Lena, can you open us in prayer? I want to make sure we use this ministry as He leads."

She nods and closes her eyes. "Heavenly Father, thank You for the opportunity to partner with these ladies and You. We want to pour love and wisdom into these teens. Help direct our steps and theirs. May our conversation make You smile. In Christ's name, amen."

Sabrina echoes her agreement and looks to me. "So, any ideas on what amazing truths you want us to pass on to the girls?"

There's another folder under the picture one, and I pull it out. "I've been praying about it, and I feel like we're supposed to focus on their identity in Christ. They are all ninth-graders in new buildings or schools. It's likely the girls are unsure of themselves and vulnerable to following crowds who will lead them down destructive paths."

Lena nibbles on her lower lip. "Been there."

You're Brilliant

"It's heartbreaking how many have. I'd like us to think of projects and discussions that hammer the fact they are beloved daughters of the King of Kings. They are beautiful. Amazing. Brilliant."

My hand shakes a little as my pen waits for inspiration. I remember gym class in high school. The locker rooms. The cliques. But just as unnerving, the memory of those sixth graders holding up those banned books full of half-dressed models and demonic titles, ugh. *I'm not feeling the brilliance.*

Lena picks up her phone for some Google research when out of the corner of my eye I catch a group of familiar-looking students. Their neon-colored crocs. The high-pitched laughter as they reach for their to-go cups and shake their messy buns held by scrunchies. Behind them, a few boys push through wearing blue and gold football jerseys. Their grunts and cheers seem to be magnets for the girls, escalating their giggles. A couple in the rowdy group I recognize from the milk melee my first day.

"Mom, you okay? Lena just asked a question." Sabrina waves with one hand while rubbing my arm with the other.

My focus remains on the kids, although I chuckle. "Sorry. I'm scatterbrained today. What were you saying?" The boy with glasses who slid through the milk locks eyes with mine, and his smile disappears. He tilts his head, nudges his friends, and points my way.

Lena speaks, but her voice sounds far-off.

The students cluster in a semi-circle and their united stare prompts me to stand. "I'm sorry. Excuse me for a moment." My feet feel like I have cement block shoes instead of heels as I approach the middle schoolers.

The boy drops his arm to his side. His eyes narrow. "You're the lady from Cafeteria-geddon."

My skin starts to itch. "Yes. It looked like you were staring at me. Is there something I can help you with?"

The girl next to him with caramel-colored hair rolls her eyes. "My mom said I came home smelling like baby spit-up thanks to you."

There's a heat burning from the top of my head, and it's spreading like a forest fire. Instead of tea, I not only want to drink ice water, I'd like to dive in some. "I apologize. The cafeteria incident was an accident."

The young man with glasses shakes his head. "No. The real accident was Principal Tucker hiring you."

You're Brilliant

CHAPTER FIVE

Bethany

The only thing I'm looking forward to Wednesday is the Linked meeting. First, I need to complete a full day of school without landing in the principal's office. My dad drops me off, and KJ is at the entrance, arms folded, waiting.

My steps toward her are as fast as the time I had to run to the bathroom but my foot got stuck in a wad of gum. "Hey. Got your text. I would have responded but my mom took my phone away."

She looks to the ground before replying, her voice quiet, but steady. "Did Sully start it, or did you?"

The warning bell sounds, so I head up the stairs toward the entrance. And KJ with her long legs strides right next to me. With each foot forward, I quietly pray for the words to say. No girl wants someone to trash talk their boyfriend, but I'm not lying either.

KJ reaches out and touches my arm. "It's okay. Just tell me."

I sigh and head up the stairs toward our lockers. "It wasn't so much him as all of them. They tried to get me to leave the table I was at."

We reach my locker, and KJ lingers. "So, he wasn't the culprit?"

I mean yeah, but… "It was a group thing."

Her stance relaxes and she reaches out for a quick hug. "Thanks, Bethany. My parents said if he was the bully, I had to break up with him."

My stomach drops to the floor. Forget school. I want to climb in the locker and live there. "KJ, he treats you okay, right?"

Her jaw lowers, but KJ doesn't speak. In fact, she doesn't move.

I swing the locker door back and forth to grab her attention. "Hey. Has he hurt you in any way?"

KJ blinks a few times and waves her hands. "No, Bethany, no. He's great. Sully's the best. My parents made me ask you. I knew it was the other guys. I think I'll be in your lunch period today, so we can sit together. Sully's suspended, so you don't have to worry."

She jogs off while I stand still, watching her. *God, you've got to help me. I think Sully's worse than a bully. I think he's an abuser.*

It's always easy to find where the Linked meeting is because the pizza and brownie aromas entice us before we even reach the top of the stairs to the youth area. Jazmin races past me and bursts through the side room where the smells trigger my hunger pangs. I walk through and see Ms. Cheri setting out plates. Something's missing, though. She's got all the chips and drinks. Napkins and cups. But there's no smile.

"Ms. Cheri, everything okay?" I put my phone down on the table and give her a hug.

She drops a plastic plate as her arms wrap around me. "How can I not be? My girls are here for my favorite ministry." Our leader returns to set-up, but something's off. I look around to see Sabrina entering, and Jazmin and Hayley are seated. Do I try to talk to Ms. Cheri? Is now a good time to let her know my concerns about KJ?

Jade storms in like a blast of cold air. "I hope there's coffee because I need caffeine. School is killing my energy." The former mean girl plops in her seat and runs a recently manicured hand through her sleek black hair, also newly colored.

Hayley, in her long tunic sweater and leggings, shoots her a look full of confusion. "We've barely had school. Why are you so tired?"

Jade expels a dramatic sigh. "This girl needs her beauty sleep. All summer I slept until noon. This six business is for the birds." On that, we all agree.

Ms. Cheri completes her plate set-up and joins the rest of us. "Change is hard. That's for sure, Jade."

Jazmin nudges me and mouths, "She okay?"

I shrug. When I woke up, the only person I was worried about was myself. Now there's KJ and Ms. Cheri.

Sabrina's the last to enter, nearly floating through the entry with her contented smile and small flash from her sensible ring. "Finally! I've waited all summer for Linked to start up again!"

We jump up and run to the mentor closest to us in age. She takes our hugs in as a group, and then we return to our seats.

Cheri takes a breath and glances around the room. "I feel the same way. Lena, Sabrina, and I are so excited to have Linked starting up again. We have a lot of plans for the school year. We know you have changes in your lives. We do, too. So let's start with the most important thing—prayer. Lena?"

Lena nods and bows her head. "Heavenly Father, thank You for new beginnings. We ask your blessing on this new season of Linked. Give us great experiences and conversation that bless Your name. Guide us as leaders. Help us all stay healthy. Protect us all from temptation, especially the distractions that creep up when we try to plan or go to Linked events. Let everything we do bring You glory. In the precious name of Jesus, Amen."

We lift our heads with a united "Amen." It's so subtle I nearly miss Cheri swiping the edge of her eye. She quickly recovers and pastes on a wide smile I realize I've taken for granted. "Okay, girls. Help yourselves to the refreshments. I know I'm ready to inhale that pizza. Once we finish, I'm going to talk a bit about labels."

Jazmin's the first in the refreshment line. "Like the brand of shoe or jeans we wear?"

Lena takes a place in line and shakes her head. "You'll see." She winks.

Once seated, Hayley scoots her chair closer to me. "Did you get in a lot of trouble for the whole cafeteria thing?"

Cheri holds her pizza mid-air as she hears Hayley. Pretty sure she'll be asking me about that later.

"I have detention, but my parents and the school understood the instigators were the guys. Speaking of, that girl from student council who helped me? KJ? She's dating one of them, and I get a really bad vibe about how he treats her."

Jazmin's milk chocolate-colored eyes widen. "Like how?"

I wait to swallow my pizza. "She was insistent I tell her if Sully started it. If so, her parents were going to make her dump him."

Hayley gasps. "Sounds like a great guy."

"Thing is, he's a bully. I think he's as awful with KJ as he was with me."

By now, Jade slides her chair closer. "What's going on?"

Hayley wastes no time catching her former nemesis up. "Bethany thinks a girl at her new school is dating a bully."

Jade shifts in her chair and looks to the floor. "Not everyone is bad news."

I give her a gentle nudge. "Hey, I know that. And you're not like that anymore, so don't feel bad."

It's refreshing to see her defeated look disappear as we nod. Her posture straightens and a spark returns to her emerald-colored eyes. "Thanks." She turns to me. "What does this guy do that has you wondering?"

The picture of his much larger frame moving in on my space with his mocking tone makes me want to stop eating. "He knows he's physically intimidating and I think he takes advantage of that. He also enjoys making fun of people."

Hayley clears her throat. "You know, now I'm concerned. You made him look stupid and refused to obey his commands."

Right. His hot glare nearly branded my skin. "Not just him, his minions too."

Jade rolls her eyes and blows at her bangs. "I know what she's getting at. Bethany, someday this guy is going to be off suspension. And more than likely, ready to come after you."

You're Brilliant

CHAPTER SIX

Cheri

Usually these twenty-five women with their notepads open and coffee cups filled give me the energy to teach their Sunday school class. As all eyes rest on me, I still can't shake what the teen said to me a few days ago at Mugs. The load of not only feeling like a disappointment but being told I was a failure grows within me, and the notes I have in front of me might as well be in hieroglyphics. *Lord, need some help here. I can't seem to focus.*

Violet West, Jazmin's grandmother with a connection to the Almighty, which most think is intuition, stands and walks over to me. "Can I pray for you?"

I nod, barely able to whisper my thanks as I close my eyes and lift surrendered hands. Ms. Violet's prayer wraps me in comfort and peace. The dryness in my throat disappears, and so do the jumbling thoughts that started with those teens and worsened with my own negative self-talk.

She finishes and gives my hand a reassuring squeeze. "You taught us never receive defeat from the enemy of our soul because he's a liar. And, he's the real defeated one. Not us. Not you."

Usually Sabrina's the one to use my own words to encourage me. Violet's reminder slams into my soul and rests. I hug her and look again at the notes. Time to teach.

By the time the service starts, I'm excited to worship and hear my husband's message. As the praise team starts with "Raise a Hallelujah," Chet takes my hand and leans in. "You okay?"

I nod, looking forward to telling him at lunch how prayer changed the message I've been listening to all week. Failure, disappointment, and worthless won't be found in God's dictionary. *Thank You, Lord, for being my peace.*

You're Brilliant

Chet begins the sermon after the offering, and he looks extra distinguished with his new glasses. "My dad was a farmer. He grew up with rooster wake-up calls and chores that involved shoveling manure." He pauses as chuckles fill the air. "I also believe with his line of work, he had sayings that might have started on the farm, but came to mean other things. Today, I'm talking about foxes in the hen house."

Even though Chet read sermon highlights to me, I lean in with my notebook and pen. Church has always been my personal battery charger. Now that I'm also working at the middle school, I need to be as equipped as ever.

"Jesus actually talks about a fox and a hen in Luke thirteen. If you open your Bibles to verses thirty-one through thirty-five, you'll see. You'll also notice He isn't talking about a literal fox. Nor is He referring to an actual hen."

There's a few whispers behind me. I turn just enough to see Hayley from the corner of my eye, and Jazmin trying to shush her. Most likely a case of not understanding the verse, or where to find it.

Nothing distracts Chet. "A lot of us are in situations we don't understand. We search for purpose. Perhaps, God's plan for you is to be the mama hen. I don't care who you are or what you do, sneaky foxes are everywhere."

My mind wanders as I consider the students I've crossed paths with in the cafeteria and library. Their bold shirts and trendy jeans mask their insecurities. The withdrawn kids who nap during lunch because the fighting at home kept them up. The girls sharing way too much of themselves through their phone in hopes of positive attention from someone, anyone.

"Foxes in a henhouse are not about setting up a home with the hens and making a peaceful life together. Foxes come to slaughter." A chorus of "Amens" rise as I re-focus on the message.

A chill runs up my spine as I think about the headlines, even local ones. We have traffickers active in the area because Route 80 can take victims across the country before law enforcement can track them. There have been funerals in our sanctuary, where we said goodbye to beloved people who lost their lives to addiction.

"If you're Christ-followers, can you do something to protect the hens that have been entrusted to you? That's what Jesus did. He laid His life down when the fox came. We are the hens that were due for slaughter. Am I saying die to your cause or purpose? No. But I am challenging you to consider your perspective. Maybe you're being called to protect the hens."

A teenaged voice blurts out "woah" blurts out behind me, followed by, "Bethy, you okay?"

I make a note to check on Bethany.

As the soft keyboard music begins, I reflect on the message. Am I at the middle school for more than making some extra money for the wedding? Do I have a call to protect the children? Already they're subject to inappropriate books and horrific websites in the school and when doing research. I need to switch gears about why I'm there and stop dreading it because I don't know where I fit in. There's a need for me to fill. This Mama needs to watch over the hens.

After service, Chet disappears into the lobby. My purse and coat still remain in the sanctuary, so I linger, wishing Mrs. White a happy birthday and laughing at Mr. Keith's latest dad joke. Bethany stands behind him, tapping her foot and looking around.

"Sweetheart, did you need to talk?" My hope is that, if I address the teen, Mr. Keith will go on his way and give us girls privacy.

He does just that, and Bethany closes the gap between us. "Mrs. Cheri, do you think we have foxes at school?"

We sit down and face each other. *Father, give me the words.*

"Absolutely. In fact, as Pastor shared, I felt God giving me a nudge to be a mama hen at the middle school. There's a lot of vulnerable kids I can pray for or talk to before they fall into trouble."

She nods, her ponytail bobbing. "Can someone my age be a protective hen?"

I look into those compassionate eyes of hers. "Yes, but within reason. Is there something going on at school?"

"There's this girl who has been helping me adjust to school. She has a boyfriend, and he's bad news. But I think it's more than being obnoxious, which he is. I think he's abusive."

The word pounds into my chest with the impact of a lead ball. "This is a situation that should involve your teacher and guidance counselor. You're a great friend, Bethany, but this isn't something you should handle yourself."

She looks to the ground. "KJ really likes him."

I place my hand on her arm. "Can I pray for you?"

Another bob from her ponytail.

"Heavenly Father, thank You for sending Your son to us to protect us. There's so much evil in the world, and in our own strength, we can't do a thing. I ask that You give Bethany your wisdom and discernment. Guide her path so she can be a friend, but be protected. Keep her friend invisible to the enemy. For this young man, I ask that he realize his choices are not good ones and that he finds help sooner than later. Surround the school with Your protection. We give You the glory. In Christ's name, Amen."

Bethany jumps up and throws her arms around me. "I knew you'd make me feel better. Thanks, Mrs. Cheri. I hope your school week is the best yet."

She's off before I can reply. I look up and notice Chet on his way toward me. Now that the service is over and he's finished socializing, it's lunchtime.

"Hey, hon. How was it?" Chet reaches for my coat and helps me put it on.

"Amazing. Bethany Tuttle visited with me for a bit to learn more."

He faces me, his eyes wide with surprise. "Really? Praise God." He hands me my purse and reaches for my hand. "How about you? Did the message speak to you in any way?"

The force I felt in my chest still radiates. "Funny you ask. I think my place at school is the same as Linked."

"Meaning?"

"I'm a mama hen assigned to the school to watch over those precious hens. And the foxes are already in the building, circling."

You're Brilliant

CHAPTER SEVEN

Bethany

With Sully and his buddies suspended, school is much easier to endure. KJ and I sit together at lunch and she's introduced me to her other soccer and student council friends. I'm the only freshman at the table, and not gonna lie, it feels pretty sweet.

"Hey, KJ, is Sully allowed to go to the homecoming dance?" MacKenzie, a sophomore with bright red hair and a lot of freckles, nudges our tall friend.

She shrugs and focuses on her milk straw. "He thinks so. Coach is working the school hard to make sure he plays the game, so I guess the dance would be included."

Logan, a petite soccer player with intense blue eyes that make her almost look like a sweet anime cartoon, leans across the table to steal one of KJ's fries. "Have you seen him since the suspension?"

Please don't look at me. Don't anyone blame me for his absence.

"Yeah, a couple times. I've been busy with soccer, though." She doesn't look at any of us, just keeps playing with the straw.

Shelane, a cheerleader who also is part of student council, expels one of those dreamy sighs I see on TV when I watch a rom com. "KJ, you sound like you're talking about a dead pet. You're dating Brent Sullivan. He's super popular and hasn't even reached upper class yet. He's only going to get more popular. That means by association, so will you."

KJ rolls her eyes and glances at me. "Bethany, are you settling into school okay?"

I wipe my mouth with my napkin and clear my throat, trying to find an answer that can steer the girls away from talking about Sully.

"Getting there. Thanks for the head's up about Mr. Marshall's long pauses. Just when I think he's done talking, he decides to continue."

Everyone chuckles and I want to let out a sigh of relief that matches Shelane's dramatic one. Before I have the chance, Shelane faces KJ. "Seriously, girl. I'm trying to tread lightly, but let me throw it to you so you don't miss it. Sully's a hot property. I know a couple girls who were circling around after the first game. I'm just saying appreciate what you have before he's gone."

I don't know where to look or if I should even move. Given the frozen looks on MacKenzie and Logan's faces, they must be as stunned as I am. Shelane puts everything on her tray and leaves for the receptacle.

This time KJ exhales for drama. She stands and waits for Shelane to return for her backpack. "Shelane. I'm aware of what I have. Just know sometimes the packaging is a lot nicer than what's found inside." She turns to me. "See you in Spanish."

It remains awkward as KJ marches off, and Shelane leaves without saying another word. Pastor Chet's words come to mind. Foxes circle the hen house. This school is full of trouble, and the common denominator seems to be Brent Sullivan.

With school finally done for the day, Mr. Burke calls my name over the loudspeaker, which interrupts my lazy plan to go home and watch YouTube videos. KJ's next to me in health and she raises an expertly crafted eyebrow.

"Are you in trouble again?"

I think back to the last few days. "Not that I know of. Guess I'll catch you tomorrow."

She smiles as I gather my things. "Good luck."

It takes two minutes to reach the office and Mrs. Erickson greets me with a hello, giving no hint that I'm about to be punished. "Bethany, how do you like Boardman Valley?"

"Well, the part where I get called down here by Mr. Burke isn't that fun, but KJ has been a great help."

Mrs. Erickson puts her hands to her heart. "That girl is such a blessing. The best babysitter. Great soccer player. My son-in-law wants her to play basketball, but so far, she hasn't expressed interest."

Funny. The other day she mentioned how much she loves playing after dinner with her dad.

Mr. Burke opens his door and those pursed, dry lips making me wonder if he's trying to smile. "Ah, Miss Tuttle. Come in. I have a proposal for you."

Well this sounds interesting.

He gestures for me to enter, and I take the first chair across from his desk. He moves some folders around and clasps his hands. "Your teachers are impressed with you. They find you smart, but also witty. I've seen some of that humor, and I'd like to steer it in the right direction."

Where is he going with this? I avoid his gaze and focus on my fading nail polish. "What are you thinking?"

"The fall play is shorter than previous years. I'd like you to form a group and perform a comedy sketch before each performance. Something akin to an opening act."

You're Brilliant

A slideshow of my favorite comedians' races through my imagination. "You mean like a SNL skit?"

Mr. Burke straightens. "What is SNL?"

"Saturday Night Live. The TV show. Chevy Chase, Eddie Murphy, Adam Sandler…"

He holds up a hand as soon as I utter Sandler. "Oh, no. That's not what I'm thinking. Their routines are wildly inappropriate. Think puns and corny. A ten-minute warm-up routine. Tops." More pushing the folders around. "I would of course approve the script beforehand."

Of course. Still, this is the best thing I've dealt with since meeting KJ. I stand and put on my backpack. "Thanks for thinking of me, Mr. Burke. I won't let you down."

Mr. Burke keeps his gaze on his desk as I walk toward the door. "Happy to hear it, Miss Tuttle. Have a good evening."

"You too." I sing, tempted to dance down the hall as I prepare to leave for the day.

Instead, I adopt a brisk pace as I find KJ at her locker. She raises an eyebrow, but doesn't speak. I'm ready to tell her all about my comedy group when there's a vibrating noise, and KJ slides her phone out of her backpack with the stealth of a trained spy.

It's my turn to raise an eyebrow. I glance over and can clearly see a face on her screen, revealing a call. It's Sully.

CHAPTER EIGHT

Cheri

After six weeks on the job, the cold, brick school building doesn't send my stomach into a tsunami of nerves anymore. The construction still isn't finished, so Principal Tucker continues to shuffle me around. The front desk receptionist thinks she has the flu, so I'm the smiling face the tired students get to see this dreary Monday.

"Good morning! Hey, I like that hat." I try with every middle schooler passing my window to offer a warm greeting. The response is deafening silence. I'd give anything to have the Linked girls still here.

Sabrina rushes into the copy room across from my area with a quick hello.

The only physical movement I see is answering the phone and greeting visitors, so I join her. "Can I help?"

She pushes a strand of hair behind her ear. "I wish. We're supposed to have a field trip tomorrow and four students didn't bring their permission slips that were due today. All year I've been trying to teach them responsibility."

I bite my lip. How many nights had Chet and I stayed up late praying Sabrina would master organization and time management? "Are they allowed to go?"

She holds up the warm papers fresh off the printer. "If they bring these back. I have to return to class. Have a great day. Love you!"

Her affection gives me the courage to stand near the entrance and greet more students before the final bell. Sure, some mumble, others avoid eye contact, but Chet's sermon replays in my mind. I need to protect the kids from the foxes. And loving them has to come first.

By lunch time, the tardy sheet is full and I signed in six guests. Sheila, the attendance monitor, enters the reception area carrying a folder with random papers sticking out. "Cheri, do you mind calling everyone on the absentee list? I have a script written out. Chances are you'll get voicemail anyway."

I nod and take the folder. "Seems easy enough."

She offers a thin smile. "If you finish before sixth period, Mr. Tucker wants an auto call and email sent to the sixth graders about the lice incident. He said he'd email that information to you, but in case he forgets, I printed it out. It's inside the folder, on top."

There seems to be a lot of work suddenly appearing on my temporary desk. "Do I have a list of those students somewhere?"

Sheila looks at her nails before glancing at me. "I printed them out and placed them in the folder. They are all on spreadsheets." With that, she clicks down the hall with her fancy heels, leaving me just a bit overwhelmed.

A cup of hot tea seems like a good way to tackle the project, so I prepare the hot drink. *Father, help me do a good job. Amen.* With tea and prayer out of the way, I open the folder and try to discern what a spreadsheet is.

With printouts spread across my desk, I have the phone receiver in hand, ready to dial, when there's a skirmish coming toward me.

The shrill, adult voice reaches the reception area first. "Nevaeh Jackson, you were not given permission to leave the class."

A girl with beautiful braids but a scowl storms up to my open window. "I need to call my Nana."

I start to hand the phone to her when the teacher catches up. Miss Jettison, who looks irate with that vein in the middle of her forehead looking like it's about to pop. She faces the student with wide, angry eyes. "You aren't calling anyone. March back to class, young lady."

The receiver stays in my hand as I stand. Do I get Mr. Tucker? Call 9-1-1? This is new territory.

The scowl doesn't flinch. "I will not. What kind of teacher announces a gift exchange and doesn't include everyone?"

Miss Jettison looks like she was slapped. She seems to remember they are in the hallway as she glances at me and lowers her voice. "Nevaeh, you don't know all the details. Heather was in the bathroom. It was an oversight."

Nevaeh folds her arms across her chest. "You didn't make it right. No teacher should make a student cry. And when another student tries to help, that adult shouldn't discipline them. And you know my Nana don't play, so when I tell her—"

With the receiver back in the cradle, I wave my hands. "Miss Jettison, would it be okay if Nevaeh sits with me for a while? I'd love to chat and get to know her better. I promise she'll make up her work and be in next period class."

Nevaeh drops her arms to her sides with softened features. "Can you have Heather join us? I want to make sure she's okay."

I look over to the teacher, who nods.

Situation diffused. Miss Jettison marches back to her English class, and I buzz for Heather to come to the front desk. Once she arrives, her eyes swollen yet brightened at the sight of Nevaeh, the two join me.

"So it seems as if you're having a tough afternoon, girls."

Heather looks to her friend. "I went to the rest room and my locker. I came back and learned Miss Jettison announced a project for

Thanksgiving. They all drew names where the person has to create something that states all the things they are grateful for, and do it with the person they picked."

"And you knew you didn't have a person to create a project for."

Heather nods, and I notice Nevaeh's nostrils flare. "She wouldn't even let us re-draw names. I knew there was a name not picked." She glances over and I note Nevaeh swipes her hand across her cheek and lowers her head.

Now it makes sense.

I pat Heather on the arm. "Sweetheart, you're a great friend. I'm sure Miss Jettison wishes she'd done things differently. The bell's going to ring in a couple minutes. Why don't you head back?"

The girl with a high ponytail and black hoop earrings grins. "Thanks. And Nevaeh? I'd never let anyone forget you. You're way too fun."

That brings the brightest smile yet. Nevaeh turns her chair toward me once Heather is out of sight. "She's all right. So glad to know someone has my back."

Her forehead lines tell stories of pain and rejection. She puts her head down on the spreadsheets for a moment before lifting it up. "Did you know my name is heaven backwards?"

I nod. "It's beautiful. Just like you."

She recoils at the word "beautiful."

"My mama said if she'd known what hell her life would be with me, she would have named me something else. Nice, right? Just like Jettison."

My heart cracks as she confesses. How can people be so cruel? Then I think back to all the tears Sabrina cried over her parents, their addictions, and choices. Hurt people hurt people.

"I wish the world realized how our words can bring life or death." I rest my hand on her arm. "Sweet girl, you are precious. I'm so sorry your name wasn't picked, and I'm certain Miss Jettison will make it right. You're welcome to visit me anytime you're having a tough day."

Nevaeh straightens, the beads in her braids clicking together. "I'm sorry, I don't know your name."

"Mrs. Wayson. When I'm not here, I'm a pastor's wife who leads a group called Linked. Girls your age meet up once a month with ladies from the church. We talk, eat snacks, make crafts."

The bell rings, and she stands. "I'd love that, Mrs. Wayson. Thanks for everything. I feel better. I'll stop back and get info about your group soon." She waves, and my heart fills with compassion and thankfulness. Today's the first day I feel like I truly made a difference.

Two hours later, I place the papers back in the folder, ready to call Sheila when the phone rings. The ID displays Sheila. "Oh hi. I was just about to call you."

She wastes no time getting to the point. "Cheri, why is Courtney White's mother calling me about her being absent? She's in school."

I remember calling that family. Wait. I open the folder and shuffle through the papers. My hands shake as I realize what I've done. Before I can answer, the phone displays another call coming through. Another call on line three. Red flashing lights revealing multiple calls coming through make the base look like a Christmas tree. "Um, Sheila? Can I talk to you after school?"

You're Brilliant

My heartbeat races just like the time I drank three sweet teas in an hour. I pick up the phone and listen to a parent ask me why I'm calling when their kid is in school. Then answer another just like it. My email inbox notification dings. Thirty messages. The subject line all about lice and not their kid.

CHAPTER NINE

Bethany

KJ holds her phone in place while it continues to vibrate, showing Sully's arrogant face across the home screen. She starts to open her mouth, but closes it.

"Aren't you going to answer?"

She glances at the display, and then to me. "I'll call back when I get home." KJ slams the locker door, and strides for the stairs.

I raise my eyebrows as we walk in rhythm. "Sully strikes me as someone who wants your undivided attention."

We reach the first level and KJ stops near a drinking fountain. "I don't really want to talk about it. Even if that's true, the last thing he wants to hear is that when he called, I was hanging with you." She takes a drink and wipes her mouth with her sleeve. "I've got practice, and I don't want to fight with you. What did Principal Burke want?"

Oh, right. The comedy troupe. My shoulders relax at the change in topic. "The fall play needs an opening act. He asked me to create a comedy sketch."

KJ grins. "For real? You could be the next Kate McKinnon."

"That's what I thought. Principal Burke said anything resembling *Saturday Night Live* would be inappropriate. I have to hand in everything for approval."

"Ugh. Always restrictions. Listen, I have to go. Text me later." With that, KJ waves and jogs toward the locker room.

Is it wrong to pray that KJ plays so hard she tires herself out and doesn't have the energy left to call Sully back?

You're Brilliant

A week later, the final announcements include a reminder that auditions for a comedy team are happening behind the auditorium stage. A mix of excitement and terror flow through my veins, not sure if anyone will even show, or if they do, will they entertain?

KJ knows I'm stressed and walks with me to the stage. A natural leader, she offers pointers to survive the meeting. "Bethany, the kids auditioning are just as nervous as you are. Look for the ones who aren't afraid to project their voice and greet you with their eyes."

I absorb her advice, taking slow breaths in hopes of calming my soaring heart rate. "What if the people who do that aren't funny?"

She bites at her lip for a moment before snapping her fingers. "Make them the straight man."

When we part, I march backstage to find Mr. Walsh, my History teacher, with an iPad in one hand while he points with his other. "Hey, Bethany. Mr. Burke asked me to oversee this venture. It's technically a drama department project, but Miss Briggs is tied up with the play. She gave me a key to the backroom and told me to hold the auditions there." He digs in his pocket and produces it. "Want to open up? I'll direct the students to the room."

I take the key and approach the door. I'm pretty new to the school and don't know a lot about the drama department, but as I wiggle and maneuver to get inside, the small area backstage. The door finally budges and the stale aroma greets me before I even step in. It's like my grandma's attic kind of a smell.

I turn on the light switch, but it doesn't help the atmosphere. Instead of a meeting room, it's basically a closet space with room for an old desk crammed in the back, two chairs, and enough floor space for four people to stand. Tops. No windows, nothing colorful or with pizzazz like I associate with plays. If there's going to be anything fun around, it absolutely has to come from the students.

"Is this the place for comedy?" A female voice behind me sounds disgusted more than questioning.

I turn and find a girl I've seen with pink hair. "Joke's on us, right?" My laugh is as lame as the room.

She takes out her phone. "It's a closet."

Can't argue with her on that. "I'm Bethany Tuttle. Mr. Burke asked me to set this up. Mr. Walsh should be here in a minute."

Another set of footsteps approaches. MacKenzie, my lunch partner with the tomato-red colored hair, stops behind pink hair. "What, did you lose a bet to be stuck in this space?"

This time I laugh out loud. I don't recall her being that funny at lunch, but then again, we're usually listening to Shelane talk all things boys and cheerleading. "Hey, MacKenzie, I'm happy to see you." I turn to the new girl. "I'm sorry, your name is?"

"Darcy. A couple of my friends said they were coming, too. I have my act on my phone. I'm going to look it over while we wait."

MacKenzie and I exchange looks as Darcy goes over her lines. She seems professional and serious about the auditions, possibly better prepared than I am.

"KJ told me that you're looking for a group that will perform each night before the fall play?"

I nod. "Right. If there's a big enough group, he said we can form one under the drama department and even have our own show. I'm just trying to get through today."

You're Brilliant

MacKenzie cracks her knuckles. "You'll be fine. You're funny, and I'm sure picking out a team won't be hard."

Two guys knock on the door and approach the threshold. "Is there even room for us to come in?"

Darcy looks up and waves them in. "These are the friends I was talking about." She points as they shuffle in. "Jeff. Craig."

I move to the desk and sit on top of it. It wobbles, and I'm sure there's an inch of dust on my jeans. "Thanks for coming. Mr. Walsh should be here any minute. If you want to go over your material while you wait, feel free."

My prediction is accurate as our advisor waltzes in, his brown eyes widen as he inspects the room. "I knew this wasn't going to be the best place in the school, but wow this is small. Miss Briggs needs the stage and back for her rehearsal and set design work. I guess we'll have to make due." He shimmies his way to the chair next to the desk. "Let's give it two minutes and we'll begin. Bethany, if you could share your vision for the fall performances, which would be a great way to start."

MacKenzie seems laser-focused on our late twenty-something single teacher. "Will everyone make it, or will there be cuts?"

I look to the adult and he smiles as he clicks on his iPad. "Let's see what we have to work with first."

In the brief moment while we wait, I breathe in and silently pray for peace and direction. Before I can think of an "Amen," someone in screeching footwear stops at the threshold.

"Is it too late to audition? Sorry, I had to get my guitar from my car." The guy with a husky voice steps forward, revealing a tall, muscular frame wearing a football letterman's jacket. His rusty colored curls look familiar.

Mr. Walsh glances up. "Brandon Perry. Good to see you back from suspension."

The athlete lets out a nervous laugh. He tilts his head and points at me. "You're the freshman from the cafeteria."

The memory rushes back. There was Sully, No-Neck, and Guy to the Right. Looks like Guy to the Right, also known as Brandon, wants to audition. Great.

You're Brilliant

CHAPTER TEN

Cheri

I enter the church sanctuary bone tired and emotionally depleted. Throughout the last two days I apologized to all the families who were told their children had lice when that wasn't the case, and asked Sheila and Mr. Tucker for forgiveness. I'm ready to hide in the pews and stay there. As a little girl I complained about always being at church as soon as the doors opened. Now? The sanctuary is my refuse.

Chet flips on the light and walks toward me without saying a word. He sits and places his hand over mine. "How can I help?"

I lean back and notice gray coming in along his temple area. And he looks so handsome. "I feel like the biggest failure. Not sure what you can do about that."

My beloved chuckles and leans back next to me, tightening his grip on my hand. "Actually, I do. First, let's look at the facts." He turns toward me. "You're an amazing wife. All the ways you take care of me? I can't even count that high."

"You have to say that. You're my husband and pastor."

He shakes his head. "No, not so. I can't lie in church. Then there's the wonderful way you stepped up to take care of Sabrina. You could have suggested she stay with someone else, or go to a foster home, but no. She has a mother in her life because of you."

I drink in the encouragement. When Sabrina moved in, she was one broken little girl who had seen too much pain and consequences from her biological addicted parents. "Sabrina has always been something special. God's hand is constantly on her."

"True. Because God's hand led her to you."

It's impossible to sulk. I straighten and lift our joined hands to my cheek. "Thank you. I just need some quiet time with the Lord. I know I'm meant to be at the school and make an impact for the Kingdom of God."

Chet places a tender kiss on my hand before releasing it and standing. "Amen. I'll leave you alone while I finish my notes for Sunday's sermon. There's about twenty minutes before the doors open for mid-week service."

"There's no Linked tonight, so I'll be here. I appreciate your support. Loving you is pretty easy, Chet Wayson."

He winks and starts for his office, his return declaration of love echoing through the pews.

With the area still and holy, I place my hands on the back of the bench ahead of me and lower my head. "Heavenly Father, I need Your guidance and peace. I feel like all I've done at the school is mess things up, but I know You called me there. I think about girls like Nevaeh and I know there's something I can offer them. Your Son. In those cold halls those students need to know they are loved. Help me."

I maintain my physical posture and wait. Of all the things my mind sees, it's upstairs. The Linked area. Not only do I picture Hayley, Jazmin, Bethany, Jade, Emily, Lena, and Sabrina, but the room is full of girls I recognize from school. A thought drops into my spirit.

Love these girls. Speak the truth. They are beautiful. Amazing. Brilliant. And so are you.

The affection I feel wrapping around me is more than Chet or Sabrina or any human could give. I gasp at the holiness and pure intimacy of the moment. "I will, Lord. Thank You for loving me, and them. I lean on Your Wisdom and discernment."

Surrender the stinkin' thinkin' my daughter.

It's such a private exchange and yet so profound, the truth sends a chill up my back.

Mr. Tucker's kind smile is the first to greet me as I enter the school doors on Monday. "Ready for a great week, Mrs. Wayson?"

I recall God's challenge to love the students. Encourage the hurting girls. "Yes. Do you have a new placement for me?"

He nods and gestures for me to follow him to his office. My gait evolves from confident pastor's wife to a baby deer hours after birth. Still, I focus on taking a deep breath and not worrying about what Mr. Tucker has in mind for me.

"Have a seat. I think you'll like what I have for you."

I pull at my skirt as I sit on the edge of the chair. "I'm game for anything."

Mr. Tucker chuckles and opens a file. "That's what I've observed. You came on board with construction in the building and confusion in the halls. You've done well trying your best and learning new skills." He pulls out a paper. "Your resume triggered an idea. You have your Bachelor's Degree, and that makes you more than eligible for the position."

If I lean any more forward in the chair, I'll fall forward. With intentional steadied breathing, I twist my wedding ring as I wait for more information. "Okay. I'm curious."

He clears his throat and slides a paper across his desk, stopping at the edge, in front of me. "It's a contract for a teacher's aide position. You have strong communication skills, and you're compassionate. I have a classroom that has a couple more students than the others, and it's not an easy group of students. The teacher and I discussed ways we could relieve some of the stress, and I thought of you."

My jaw lowers, not sure how to respond.

"A teacher's aide is exactly what the title implies. You don't need to be licensed, but you would support the teacher in group and one-on-one sessions. Your duties could include anything from taking attendance to helping students create an outline for book reports."

Wow. This feels like a promotion. "Would disciplining students be part of my responsibilities?"

"There might be an extremely rare circumstance where the teacher is out of the room and you would be in charge. For the most part, you are a good candidate for the position because you can back up Miss Jettison with encouragement and yet build up the students."

The name takes me back to the angry exchange between teacher and students over an exchange gone wrong. "Did you say Miss Jettison?"

Another nod. "You made quite an impact with two of her students. Nevaeh and Heather." He stands. "I'm going to greet students while you read the contract. If you want the position, sign, and I'll walk you to your new classroom. You'll be a perfect fit, and Ellen Jettison could benefit from your nurturing. The class is hurting, and you seem to be the healing balm they all need."

CHAPTER ELEVEN

Bethany

It's after five and my stomach launches a song to rival the volume of Jeff and Craig's kazoo duet.

Mr. Walsh stifles a yawn and scribbles some notes on a pad before looking up. "Okay. There's one act left. Brandon? What do you have for us?"

Sully's friend adjusts the guitar strap around his neck. "I like to create songs from random things."

There's a flash of something from Mr. Walsh's eyes. Interest? Curiosity? It's definitely a different look than he offered MacKenzie and her stand-up routine about study hall. Our advisor waves Brandon forward. "Go ahead."

The junior with broad shoulders and ripped muscles swallows. "Um, Bethany? Would you suggest something that's school related?"

We lock eyes. His voice squeaked at the request, making him seem a lot less intimidating than our first meeting in the cafeteria. I try to look away, but his brown eyes are as attractive to focus on as chocolate kisses. "Does lunch work?"

His hands rest over the guitar strings, leaving an awkward musical sound. He coughs and runs a shaky hand through his brown, wavy hair. "You said lunch?"

I nod and glance at Mr. Walsh, who says nothing.

Brandon closes his eyes and moves his head to a silent beat. The clock ticks and my stomach threatens to rumble in rhythm. After an extended pause, he opens his eyes, places his fingers over the strings, and starts an upbeat, country tune.

You're Brilliant

"My belly started rumblin' and the clock it struck noon----I looked to the teacher and she said, 'Boy you'll eat soon." When the bell rang, I ran down the hall---the closer to the cafeteria, I could smell it all. There were taco shells and pizza pies, and something mesquite----there were fruit cups and hot dogs and the famous mystery meat. I went to pay, saw some bananas and grabbed a big bunch----cuz it's my favorite time at school, you know it's gotta be lunch. Cuz' it's my favorite time at school, you know, you know it's gotta be luuunnnchhh!" Brandon strummed hard at the end and stopped, resting his hands at his side.

Mr. Walsh wastes no time. "Bravo. Musical improv. Risky, but entertaining. Bethany?"

I really want to dislike Brandon's audition and even him. But he's good. My friends love stuff like this. "Brandon, that was great."

He beams, and there's a bounce in his step as he places his guitar in the case. "Thanks for letting me try. I know I got in trouble recently, and I wasn't sure I'd be allowed."

"When I heard, my guess was you weren't the leader, and most likely were wishing you hadn't been there." Mr. Walsh's theory brings a slow nod from Brandon, who approaches me.

"I owe you an apology. We treated you pretty bad that day in the cafeteria. It won't happen again." He extends his hand, but pauses. "At least, not from me."

"Thanks, Brandon. I accept." We shake, and I pack up my things feeling Brandon isn't as close to Sully as I thought. And that this opening act deal might be a lot of fun.

Mr. Walsh also moves toward the door. "Bethany, compile your notes tonight and email me your thoughts by morning. I'll take them and post results on the drama board and Instagram page by the end of the day tomorrow. Then, we jump right in with the material."

There's a lot of work ahead. "Got it. I have some ideas." I step out into the backstage where Brandon waits.

"Counting on it." Mr. Walsh smiles, shutting off the lights from our little room.

"Do you need a ride? Coach let me know I could miss practice today for the audition. Season's about over anyway and we're not in the playoffs." Brandon steps next to me and matches my stride as I pass the fall play props.

I can imagine my dad's reaction if a high school junior drives me home. "Thanks, but I texted my mom. She's going to pick me up on her way home from work."

He looks at the ground.

"You did a great job with that song. It reminds me of that improv show Wayne Brady is on. I even wondered if we could structure our act around that theme." As soon as I finish speaking, Brandon raises his head and smiles.

"Awesome. Whether I get a spot or not, this was fun. The comedy sketch will be great, with opportunities to grow."

Before I can share my thoughts on using the comedy troupe to host fundraisers or open other drama club activities, a male voice booms from behind.

"Perry! Where were you today?"

Brandon and I stop and turn at the same time. His grin disappears, and I groan.

You're Brilliant

"Hey, Sully. Coach knew where I was. I tried out for the comedy troupe." His words rush out before KJ's boyfriend jogs up.

When Sully recognizes me, and looks to his buddy, the jock scowls. "You missed football to be part of some stupid group? With her?"

They both focus on me. Please don't let me sass my thoughts back, that I think football is a stupid group. I look at my phone and silently pray a text pops up that tells me my mom is waiting outside.

"Dude, you're thinking of the old days and drama clubs. It's legit now." Brandon nudges Sully with his arm. "And comedy? It's awesome."

I work once again on steadying my breathing. The last thing I want is to start trouble.

Sully cocks his head. "Seriously?" He points at me. "But this one? She's not funny. And she's certainly not cool." His eyes darken the longer he stares.

What does KJ see in this guy?

Brandon shakes his head and starts walking. "She's a freshman, sure. But it was a good time." He turns his head just enough for me to catch his wink.

My heart settles, and the phone vibrates. Thank God for Mom.

Sully moves with him. "You're not going to miss the rest of football, are you? We've got the last game."

"No way. I'm there. C'mon, I'll give you a ride home."

The two pick up their pace, and I lag behind to avoid any kind of confrontation. The one door I can use to meet mom is where the guys are headed. Once they disappear out the exit, I regain strength in my legs and arms, the first time where everything feels normal since auditions.

I reach the front entrance and push on the heavy door in hopes of spotting mom's SUV and going home. Before I find her in the parking circle, I have to pass the guys. Brandon and Sully sit on the concrete wall leading to the doors. Oh stomach, don't flip out on me now.

"See ya." My words are not much louder than a whisper, and geared more toward Brandon, but if it keeps Sully quiet on his perch, awesome.

Brandon offers a toothy smile and waves. "Thanks again, Bethany."

I return the wave and scan for mom's car. Found it.

Sully's taunting voice causes my shoulders to tense. "Hey. I still don't think you're funny, and I definitely don't like you putting ideas in my girl's head. Do me a favor and keep your distance from her. Or I'll show you what's funny."

You're Brilliant

CHAPTER TWELVE

Cheri

Each step Mr. Tucker takes toward Miss Jettison's homeroom, the more I want to announce my resignation and run home. Familiar worry lines must be creasing my tightening forehead just as it did during our first pastorate, and my perspiration-damp feet slip in my shoes thanks to the increase in moisture. Yet the principal knocks on her door and whistles as he waits.

She peeks through the slim window panes and unlocks the door, but I'm pretty sure a scowl overcomes her as I walk through.

"Miss Jettison, Cheri Wayson is your new aide. She's a perfect answer to help with your bigger class and is more than willing to offer whatever support you need."

I extend my hand to nothing but air, quickly returning my arm to my side. "It's a pleasure to work with you."

Her exhale brings the hair on my arms to a standing position as she lowers her glasses to the ridge of her nose. "Yes. I'm familiar with your work." When Principal Tucker looks away, she scratches her head.

Was that a joke about my lice email?

He returns his focus to me with a clap of his hands. "You two will be great. Enjoy the new position. Congratulations." With that, he turns on his heel and leaves.

Jesus, I really need Your help. "What can I do? Whatever you need, I'm ready."

If my smile can eradicate her pursed lips and slits for eyes, I'm all for it. She doesn't respond, but hands me a red folder marked "Attendance." I hold it up. "Thank you. I'll get right to it."

You're Brilliant

The class is so quiet it's like a remote-control pressed pause on them. Nevaeh breaks the silence with a low wave and shy smile. I return the greeting with a "hello" before opening the folder and scanning the page. The names aren't simple. "Camden Baker?"

A hand raises.

"Sadeja Dwyer? Pendelton Easling? Marquis Fowler?" So far, so good. A few more F's, a G, and Murina Howard. "Ok, Nevaeh Jackson, I see you. Javon Mays? Scott Mucci? Heather Quinn?" Great, another kind, familiar face. "D'Brashia Russell?" My voice hesitates on the first name, drawing a swing of the head from Miss Jettison.

Before she says anything, a beautiful girl with layers of braids piled into a gorgeous bun speaks. "Here. But it's pronounced D'Brayja." Her tone is sweeter than I imagine the teacher's would be.

"Thank you, sweetheart." I breeze through the S's, T's, two V's, and Max Whitcomb. "J'Quon Zander?" The deep male voice responds with a "Yo." I close the folder with a sense of satisfaction. "I appreciate the help. Hopefully tomorrow I'll get all your names correct."

Miss Jettison walks past, taking the folder from me as she passes. "Class, this is Mrs. Wayson. Although she's in the classroom, remember I'm the teacher and my rules stand."

My back's turned as she utters the command, but a chill runs down my spine. No one speaks. This is no classroom, it's a holding cell. How can anyone learn here?

"Mrs. Wayson, please email the office the attendance tallies, and if the folder contains any early dismissal notes. You can handle that, correct?" Her tone is as depressing as a dreary day.

My gut feels as if I've spent the morning boxing, and losing. "I'll give it my best."

The first half of the day clicks along as I spend time listening to book reports. I meet new students as classes rotate, and a little after noon, the room is empty.

Miss Jettison reaches for a brown paper bag and shuffles through the classroom with her sensible taupe shoes. "I'm back with eighth grade honors at one-ten."

In our short time together, I gather she doesn't want to chat, or have me join her. I lock up and start to the office with hopes of running into another staff member. Before I reach the lobby, the laughs from the cafeteria tempt as much as the aroma of the sloppy Joes. With a few tentative steps, I enter the threshold. This time I don't need to duck from flying dairy products.

"Mrs. Wayson, hey!" Nevaeh stands and waves from across the room.

Okay, Lord. I'm going to love these girls like you do. Lead the way.

"Hi, everyone. How's the food?"

Neveah moves closer to Heather, making room for me. "The fries are good. Try one." Nevaeh thrusts one my way.

"Oh. Okay then." I take it and enjoy a bite. "Good stuff. So, how are things going for you all?"

Heather looks to Nevaeh, then to the girl on the opposite side. She wears her black hair short with a headband, and the glint of her eye tells me she's the adventurous one of the trio. "I'm JJ. They're trying to cheer me up because I failed my math quiz."

"You guys are good friends. That's great that you each have a support system." I face JJ. "And the praise is that it was a quiz. You can study, get a tutor, whatever you need, and be prepared for the test."

You're Brilliant

JJ rolls her eyes. "You don't know my parents. They'll ground me and I was supposed to go with these two and Heather's parents to Columbus for the weekend."

Heather sips her milk before letting out a dramatic sigh. "We have so much planned. Shopping. Swimming at the hotel. Awesome dinners."

A bit of meat falls from Nevaeh's bun, and she pushes the filling that fell out of her bun around with a fork, not making eye contact with any of us. "I've never been outside of Youngstown."

My heart is like a magnet to these three. "Have you prayed about it? None of you know for sure the trip is off. You might learn otherwise. You might not. Either way, God will direct your steps and help you all."

They exchange glances and shrugs.

"Tell you what. I'll be praying for each of you. In fact, if you're free the first Wednesday evening of the month, there are other girls just like you that we encourage and hang out with."

JJ's glint transforms into a spark. "Really? That sounds fun."

The other two nod in rhythm.

Before I'm able to continue, out of the corner of my eye I catch Miss Jettison standing at the same threshold I was at. Her arms folded and her expression is as sour as this morning. She aims her hot stare my way, and I'm wilting.

I stand, placing my hand on Heather's shoulder. "Girls, it was a pleasure to sit with you a bit. I will be praying about your trip. If you need more information about the group, Linked, let me know."

Nevaeh returns to her chair space. "I'm definitely interested."

Miss Jettison's making a beeline my way, sending me into a frenzy to finish so the girls can avoid her encounter.

"Great! I'll see you all soon." With a wave I turn and try to reach the woman first. It's a big failure. At least my back is turned to the girls when Ellen Jettison starts in.

"What are you doing? You belong in the staff lounge." Her thin eyebrows wiggle with each word.

I put my hands to my chest area. "I stopped to talk with the girls. I met JJ and learned she was having a tough day."

She expels an angry hiss. "That isn't your job. When you're at this school, you're a teacher's aide. One I'm not crazy about having in my classroom. I know about your incompetence throughout the building."

The more she talks, the more our mutual height seems to change. I think I'm shrinking into a middle school girl myself. My stomach tightens and I forget to breathe.

"Mrs. Wayson, a teacher's aide isn't a pastor's wife. I know that's your real job. But I refuse to let you come in here and throw your Jesus all over the place with my students."

My mouth lowers. My jaw locks. My knees tremble. This woman is the vortex of brokenness.

"Now, when it's lunch period, if you brought something, go to the lounge and enjoy. If you need to buy food, do so and go to the staff area like I've directed." She holds a bony finger close to my nose. "But whatever you do, don't socialize with the students and proselytize Jesus. Is that clear?"

My throat's robbed of moisture and there's probably a lack of oxygen to my brain. All I can choke out is, "Crystal."

You're Brilliant

CHAPTER THIRTEEN

Bethany

Midnight is closing in and I'm still exchanging emails with Mr. Walsh. We agree that although the auditions showed different levels of talent, it was worth accepting everyone. If only we could land on a theme for the fall sketch. His last email proposed a vaudeville act, an idea that's as popular as broccoli casserole for lunch.

"Bethany, are you still up?" Dad's footsteps come closer until he reaches my doorway. "You have school tomorrow."

I'm sprawled on the bed with the laptop and my phone. "Busy night. Even if I wanted to sleep, I don't think I can."

My confession seems to give him the green light to move my desk chair closer to the bed and sit. "School work or the drama stuff?"

Ugh. I haven't even thought about homework since dinner. "The comedy sketch is most of it. I had another run-in with that jock. KJ and I were texting a little earlier, I was hoping to hear from her before I get ready for bed."

"She's the friend dating the athlete, right?"

I nod, thinking about her last text. *Sully's fun. It's crazy that a junior likes me.*

"Bethy, you can't make her see the truth. But if he is truly a bully, it is your duty to report him to the proper adults."

I grab my pillow and scream into it. "Dad, I don't know. He makes threats, but he comes off as all talk. KJ's resistant. I don't want to lose her as a friend." Sully's last words to me bounce through my mind. *Stop hanging with KJ or else.* I toss the pillow aside.

Dad leans forward in the chair. "Have you prayed about it?"

Gulp. Why is it the first thing I should do often turns out to be the last?

He grins and clears my bed, putting everything on my desk. "Then you have a plan after I turn the lights off." He tussles with my hair and walks to the door, hitting the light switch off.

"Goodnight. Thanks for the help."

Dad's reply comes through the other side of my closed door. "Hey, I appreciate you talking to your old man."

Mr. Walsh calls me out of homeroom before I have the chance to lay my head on my desk. My exhaustion is equal parts late night and lack of breakfast. If only he'd let me sneak into the audition closet and take a nap instead of attending English.

"Bethany, good morning. I figured we could save time if we take a few minutes to hash out the play format. Then I can post the cast list."

I stifle a yawn. Must be fully alert to avoid him throwing out another vaudeville idea. "I know Mr. Burke doesn't want anything inappropriate, but Brandon's audition was fun and involved the audience."

He picks up his #1 teacher mug and takes a sip. "What are you thinking?"

Even though a few seniors enter for homeroom, I circle the front of the room, not sure how Mr. Walsh will respond. "How about a few skits like Brandon's? They don't have to all be musical, but we could have props and comments the audience writes beforehand. It could be like that improv show."

"I don't know if Mr. Burke would go for it."

With a finger snap, I move closer to the desk. "We could have you or Miss Briggs pull the best comments and put them in a hat. Same for topics Brandon could sing about. Have a few to choose from each night, but he won't know what ones. You will."

A slow smile forms. "That show is hilarious."

Now I'm waking up. "I know, right? And we could use the whole cast. Mr. Burke wants ten minutes. We could do three sketches, ending with Brandon."

He claps his hands. "It's worth a try. I'll set a meeting with Mr. Burke during my break, and if all goes well, I'll have it posted by the end of the day. How would we rehearse?"

"At least for tonight we could have everyone pull up a couple hours' worth of the show online to see how it works. Then later in the week work on a few of the best themes from the show and write our own sketches to see what works best for the group."

"Bethany, you're a natural leader. I have a good feeling about this. You better head back to homeroom, but if the plan is approved, text the gang and have them watch the videos."

I nod as Mr. Walsh takes another sip. Considering all the comments Sully's thrown my way, encouragement from a teacher is like a glass of ice water during a drought. *Thanks, God. You really take care of every detail.*

Returning to homeroom isn't easy with the latecomers scurrying to their lockers before the bell rings. Out of the corner of my eye I spot KJ with her back up against her locker, eyes wide. In front of her is Sully's tall, intimidating frame.

"Brent, my hair is caught in the locker. Open it up." Her voice sounds strangled.

And his? "You don't tell me what to do. I asked you a question and you didn't answer. I'm waiting."

His sneer triggers an anger in me that makes our cafeteria moment look like a warm-up to the main attraction.

I move in next to him and address my friend. "KJ, give me your combination. I'll open your locker."

Her eyes dart back and forth between me and Sully. "12. 27."

Sully reaches for her waist and tugs her forward, her hair trapped in the door. "Don't say the last number until you answer me. Why didn't you answer my call?"

The bell rings, and the chaos clears, making it much easier for his torture to be discovered. "Brent Sullivan, let her go! This abuse!" Screaming comes natural because I'm scared for KJ.

KJ tries to shake her head, but winces. "Please Bethany. Don't."

Sully rams me with his elbow with enough force I lose my balance, but regain composure. "Stay out of this. Go to class."

I'm pretty sure smoke is rolling out of my ears. "Someone help!" My throat scratches as I increase the volume.

He turns and moves toward me, hands wide open ready to lunge.

"Mr. Sullivan, what is going on here?"

My knees buckle in relief as Mr. Walsh jumps between us. Sully drops his arms to his side and backs up. KJ's weeping.

Me? I'm ready to take this bully down once and for all. "He's hurting KJ. He shut her hair in the locker and pulled to make her hurt. It isn't the first time. You have to do something." My words are as fast as gunfire as Sully's face grows redder. "KJ, give me the last number."

"Three."

My fingers scroll with enough speed to create a breeze to open the door. I set KJ's long locks free. The force is so hard the door slams against the next locker.

My friend squeaks out a cry and lunges into me for a hug. "Thank you. I'm sorry I didn't listen before."

Mr. Walsh's expression softens as he watches KJ sob. "Bethany, you can take her to the nurse and make sure she's okay. Ask Mrs. Waxer to call the vice-principal and KJ's parents. They will need to fill out some paperwork and take the next steps." His eyes lower and his forehead tightens as he addresses Sully. "Which could be legal. Let's go straight to Mr. Burke's office. This abuse ends now."

You're Brilliant

CHAPTER FOURTEEN

Cheri

Lena slides a plate full of breakfast casserole next to my coffee and sits across from me at her kitchen island. Even with two busy boys the area is bright, quiet, and uncluttered.

"Thanks for coming over, Cheri. I don't get a lot of time to talk with adults. I'm glad Bryce took the kids to the Y and encouraged me to call my Linked ladies for brunch. What a blessing Sabrina can come, even if she's going to be a little late." Lena dishes up a piece of the egg and sausage dish for herself and stabs into it.

"Are you kidding? This is wonderful. It's been a stressful week, so enjoying great food with even better company is perfect." I savor the rich breakfast blend topped with French vanilla creamer.

One of her eyebrows rises. "Really? You and Pastor Chet are the picture of peace to Bryce and me."

I'm not sure if I should laugh or cry. "There are nights I just collapse on the bed in tears." Like every night this week.

Her smile fades as she places another casserole piece on her plate. "It's hard to believe. You're always smiling when I see you. Our Linked meetings are organized and so fun. You make it look easy."

"Lena, there are times when I feel so incompetent, I expect the board to fire Chet because they realize what a fraud I am. And since I've started working at the school, it's been one mishap after another." Mixed emails. Food fights. Banned books in the library. "I struggle like anyone else."

She looks to the floor and then swipes her cheek. "Have you ever had to have your kitchen ceiling replaced because the bathtub overflowed? Because I made that mess. There's also the concerned email from my son's preschool because he told his class I drink three dark beers every day." Her laugh sounds more like a choked cough.

I reach over and squeeze her hand. "Oh, honey. That had to be a misunderstanding."

"I've been known to drink three Diet Root beers. Mom stress. But his teacher needed an explanation. I sounded like an addict to his class."

Much like the chocolate stash Chet and Sabrina know not to touch. "Lena, you're doing a fantastic job. Being a mom with young children is hard. But no one expects you to be perfect."

She sniffles. Then scoffs. And breaks into a sob, covering her face with the same napkin she wiped her mouth.

I push my chair closer and rub her back. "Lena, what's going on?"

The napkin unravels and she blows her nose, lifting her head and facing me. "Cheri, I'm expecting. A complete surprise."

Okay, Lord. I need Your wisdom right now. "And you're overwhelmed."

Lena nods, with more sniffles. "And scared. The boys are so busy. Don't get me wrong, they are full of love, but it's a race all day long trying to stay ahead of them. Adding a baby to the mix when Bryce travels so much? I feel like a failure and I'm not even wearing maternity clothes yet."

Even through the tears she looks beautiful with her wide eyes and sweet giggle.

"You know who isn't surprised? God. Our Creator sees you at work with these precious boys. All your time and effort with them is amazing. And now, He's giving you a promotion. Because you've got this." I slide back in my chair. "Keep doing what you're doing and it's going to be just fine."

Lena springs up and offers a hug. "Thank you. I'm sure the Linked girls will sign up to babysit. That will help." Her face brightens as she returns to her seat and nibbles on the egg mixture.

I'm about to ask more about the pregnancy when a door opens and closes, followed by footsteps that come closer. I glance toward the foyer, wondering if Bryce and the boys are back from the Y. Instead it's Sabrina. Her face is as downcast as Lena's just was, with ruddy cheeks and bags under her eyes.

I stand and move toward the kitchen entryway. "Sabrina? Are you okay?"

She looks to Lena, and then to me, shaking her head. Her bottom lip trembles. "I think the wedding is off." Sabrina sinks into the chair I had been sitting in, her coat wading up as she sits, tucking her in like a cocoon.

Lena prepares another cup of coffee and a casserole plate, brings it to the table, returning to her chair. I sit opposite Sabrina.

"That can't be. Tell us what happened."

Sabrina sighs. "I mentioned that I'd miss Ohio once we move to Wisconsin. Charlie thought I meant I don't want to leave. I got defensive, we said things, and it ended with a door slam and me here with tears dripping on my coat."

Lena and I exchange glances and a secret smile.

"Oh, that's stress coming out." Lena says, "The wedding is six weeks away, Charlie's finishing up his degree, it's a lot for both of you. Bryce and I deal with those conflicts when we're overwhelmed."

You're Brilliant

Sabrina straightens and shimmies out of her coat. "Really? We said such negative things."

I cut a piece of the egg casserole for my adopted daughter. "As you grow together, you both will learn effective communication skills. Give yourself a little time away, go back, and share specifically how you're truly feeling. Perhaps you meant you'll be a little homesick as you get settled."

"That's exactly how I feel. Charlie took it in a completely opposite direction." She attacks the brunch food with gusto, her method of eating when stressed. "So you think we'll be okay?"

I'm about to reassure both of them when my phone vibrates. I excuse myself and look, realizing it's a text from Bethany Tuttle.

Ms. Cheri, please help. My friend KJ has a bully of an ex-boyfriend. She's a mess, I don't know what to do 🙁

CHAPTER FIFTEEN

Bethany

KJ sighs and tightens the faded pink scrunchie around her long, straight ponytail as I wait for her to finish packing up in the locker room after basketball practice. "I'm not sure, Bethany. I'm usually beat Wednesday evenings. I also don't know anyone at this Linked thing. You do."

Mrs. Cheri's advice comes to mind. *Don't push it, just invite her. Help her find a new group of people to hang out with who take her away from Sully and her memories of him.* "Don't forget when school started, you knew everyone and I didn't. I was terrified, but you helped me. Everyone called me that 'Mooove along girl.' Now they recognize me and my name for the right reasons." And that I'm the one that stood up to Sully. Twice.

KJ slips into her volleyball hoodie and reaches for her backpack. "I'm still not sure. Will they think I'm stupid?"

Not sure where she's going with this. Because she plays sports? Her hometown is different than the other Linked girls? "You're not dumb. Why do you say that?"

She starts for the double doors but stops and turns, her spin so fast her shoes almost touch mine. Her face is ruddy again, and her eyes, watery. "Does a smart girl date a guy that makes fun of them and enjoys hurting them?"

Oh. Right.

Once again, Mrs. Cheri's voice comes to mind. We all fall short. "I think you're going to be surprised. Jade comes every month and her sass tends to get her in trouble. Everyone was kind to me at Linked when they knew about the mess I caused my first day of school. We've all done things that missed the mark."

You're Brilliant

Her posture relaxes and she flashes a grin. "Okay, I'll go. They better have lots of food though. After practice, I'm always hungry."

A giggle slips out as I imagine KJ and Jazmin rushing for the snacks. "It's going to be great. You'll see."

Two days later, KJ stands at the bottom of the church staircase, looking up to the gray, heavy doors that lead to the youth wing and Linked room. She sighs as if it's time to toss a free throw. "I can sweat in front of a full gymnasium with no worries. I've given countless speeches as part of student council." Her gaze turns to me. "But this is nerve wracking."

It was a couple years ago when Linked started and I was staring at the stairs. At a church I attended and knew everyone. No wonder KJ's nervous. Even the building is new. "You aren't alone. I'll stay with you the whole time."

We take the first step together. By the third, KJ treats it like a competition and increases her speed. Twelve steps later, we're at the top, and she's beaming. "First hurdle down."

I point toward the hall. "C'mon. I smell pizza."

As soon as we walk in, Sabrina smiles and heads our way. "Bethany, so good to see you!" She offers a warm hug that is as comforting as a chocolate chip cookie right out of the oven.

"Sabrina, this is KJ Curry. She's my friend from school." I turn to KJ. "Sabrina Wayson is one of the mentors here. She's a teacher in Youngstown."

"I was actually Bethy's teacher. It's nice to meet you." As the two shake hands, KJ's eyes twinkle.

"Bethy?"

"Right, I forgot. It's my nickname. When I was a baby, Mrs. Cheri babysat a couple times and Sabrina heard my name wrong and called me Bethy. It stuck and just about everyone here and at home calls me that."

KJ shimmies her hands together with a crooked grin. "Oh, the lunch table girls will love this."

Thankfully, I know she doesn't have any malice in her. If the nickname spreads, it's just for fun. I focus on Sabrina. "What's on the agenda tonight?"

She shifts so we can see Mrs. Cheri, Lena, and the front of the room. There's a long table full of tabletop waterfalls that my mom says never last two weeks and my dad confesses those things make him run to the bathroom.

KJ taps me and raises her eyebrows.

I shrug. "Um, Sabrina, what's all that?"

She starts toward the table, gesturing us to follow. Once we reach the refreshments, she stops. "Have some pizza. I made brownies. Soon enough you'll hear about the importance of the waterfalls." With a wink Sabrina reaches for a brownie and makes her way to greet Jade.

As KJ fills her plate, Hayley and Jazmin enter, chatting away. Their banter hits my gut just a little knowing the two have all day at school to hang. Before I moved, it was the three of us.

Jazmin rushes to the pizza with hands outstretched. "So hungry." Her elbow nudges KJ, also reaching for pizza. Jazmin glances up at the tall stranger. "You're new. And have great taste in pizza."

Hayley joins our half-circle. "Bethy! So glad to see you." She wastes no time giving me a hug, but also pauses when she sizes up my friend. "Is this KJ?"

I nod. "Great guess. Hayley, Jazmin, this is KJ from school. She came here from basketball practice, so make sure she gets something to eat."

Jazmin picks up a piece of sausage pizza and places it on KJ's plate. "I just left dance practice. I respect the need to eat." In pure Jazmin style, she cracks up as soon as she finishes, making us laugh, too.

We pile on our snacks and take seats together. Both Hayley and Jazmin include KJ in conversation, asking about school and sports. Even Jade moves her chair closer to listen. When Mrs. Cheri stands, I glance over at my tall friend. She offers a thumbs up.

Our pastor's wife's blonde curls bounce as she walks to the center of the room. Her smile is the one thing we can all count on when we see her. Not once do I remember her being sad or stressed. It's comforting, actually. "How is everyone doing? I can't believe our next meeting will be our Christmas party."

Lena takes a sip of water and starts coughing. Once she recovers, she rests her elbows on the table and rests her hands on her forehead. "You're kidding? I'm not even close to being ready for the season."

Sabrina opens up a book. "Same. This is my planner. There's no room left to write. Between packing up, wedding planning, and Christmas activities, I'm overwhelmed."

Those two are really selling the joys of adulthood. "Mrs. Cheri, I brought a friend from school. This is KJ Curry."

Our leader's warm smile beats any good feeling the snacks here bring. "Welcome, KJ. I'm so glad you could join us. As you can tell, we're pretty open here. Feel free to share as little or as much as you would like."

KJ plays with her crumpled napkin. "Will do."

Mrs. Cheri moves to the waterfall table and picks one up. "Have you ever gotten so frustrated that you wondered why bother?"

All of us nod, even Sabrina and Lena.

"Me too. I'd love to tell you being a pastor's wife is glamorous, but I become discouraged like anyone else. I don't do things to be recognized, but sometimes I work really hard and don't even get a thank you. It's hard."

Hayley's chuckle sounds resentful. "Like when I clean my room. No one says anything. But if I don't do it, I hear all about it."

Jade sits forward, her face aglow with recognition. "Yes! That drives me crazy."

Mrs. Cheri returns the knick-knack to the table. "I remember one year a community organization asked if they could borrow some church items for their theater. I drove everything over. My car was full. I not only dropped it all off, I helped place everything on the stage."

"There were a lot of props from the church." Sabrina adds.

Jazmin raises an eyebrow. "What happened? Did it get stolen?"

Mrs. Cheri's laugh is as light as a pancake. "No, but it felt worse than that at the time. Chet, Sabrina and I went to opening night. I glance at the program and find a page thanking people and organizations for their donation. But not the church. Not one word."

That would burn me.

She continues. "Even worse, at the end of the play the director thanked some of those people again. One lady she brought on stage to acknowledge donated a plastic plant. And yet, the furniture and other items all came from our church."

93

KJ's eyes widen as she shakes her head. "That's terrible."

"I confess, I was angry. The nerve of them to not say anything stayed with me for days. Chet was so tired of hearing me complain that he suggested I go to the park and pray. He knows the park always calms me down."

Sabrina giggles. "True story."

Mrs. Cheri looks to Sabrina, and then back to us girls. "I drove to Lanterman's Mill and basically stomped my way to the covered bridge. I stopped in the middle and rested at the side. It was serene, everything my mood wasn't." She grows emotional as her eyes water. "I heard the waterfalls. It was the most peaceful sound. And as I listened, the Lord gave me a talking to."

Hayley, Jade, Jazmin, KJ, and I remain silent, sitting on the edge of our seats.

"He said, 'The sound of the waterfalls is My applause. Would you rather have the world's opinion, or mine?' I broke on the spot. It was there I realized everything I do is for an audience of One, for Jesus. What anyone else thinks? I can't waste time on that."

Jazmin's nod is slow. "That's deep. I like it."

Cheri slides over to the table and picks up a waterfall. Sabrina and Lena join her, and do the same. They walk over to each of us and hand us a waterfall.

"Girls, it's so hard to be your age. Sometimes it looks like no one cares, or everyone has an opinion and you feel like you're suffocating." Mrs. Cheri returns to the front. "Remember the waterfalls. Even on your worst day, the Lord is there. He's rooting for you."

Both KJ and I have similar items. A mill wheel that when turned on, has water flowing into the base, complete with water sounds.

KJ traces her finger over the base. "This is beautiful. Thank you."

Sabrina stands near us. "We hope every time you look at it, you remember how precious you are. That you are so loved. Always."

After feasting on the last of the brownies, we pack up our things. KJ spends time talking with Mrs. Cheri off to the side, and I unlock my phone to see if I missed anything. There's a text from Brandon.

I didn't know. Sorry.

That's weird. I scroll down and notice he sent a screenshot. It's a video. I open the link and discover Sully's on camera. Someone off camera appears to be asking him questions, almost interview style.

"Of all the girls in Boardman Valley to stay clear of, who is at the top of your list?"

Sully leans forward on a couch and the camera pans in. "As one of the top athletes and most popular upperclassmen in the area, I consider myself an authority on the subject. I know a lot of girls. And there are two who appear all nice and sweet, but they are trouble for a lot of reasons. Their names? KJ and Bethany."

You're Brilliant

CHAPTER SIXTEEN

Cheri

There's something in the school atmosphere that isn't day-old meatloaf or the thrill of a long weekend. It's the day before Thanksgiving break mixed with deadline. In Ms. Jettison's class, the students are tired from working on their thankful projects, and wired for time off. And that doesn't sit well with the teacher.

"Boys and girls. I meet with your parents in six hours. Please settle down so I don't have to add this issue to my conversation with them." Ellen's eyes are closed and she looks like she's practicing deep breathing.

I make sure I engage with each student by offering my kindest smile.

Eyes opened, Miss Jettison sighs. "Thank you. Now, let's get into our presentations. I'm looking for creativity in why you're thankful for the person you chose, using strong speaking skills. Remember I'm also grading your written material. That needs to be unique and well-written. This is your last big grade of the quarter, so I hope you took it seriously."

D'Brashia raises her hand. "Can I go first?"

Miss Jettison brightens. "Good for you, showing initiative. Go ahead." She sits, and I do the same, but choose a chair from across the room.

D'Brashia shuffles to the front with a purple folder. "I just want to get it over with. Anyway, I chose my grams. I live with her. My mom left when I was three. Dad's got three jobs." She delivers in a flat tone, her brown eyes empty. "My grams still works as a cashier but has a clean house and food for us. I never miss a meal. She also don't tolerate our sass. She also makes us go to church. Sometimes I'd rather sleep in, but I do like going. I know Grams is tired, but she never admits it. If someone gives her money, she spends it on us. Never on herself. She's a tough lady, and I want to be like her. I'm thankful for her."

It's quiet for a few moments as Miss Jettison marks some notes down in her folder. She looks up and offers a flat smile. "What adjectives would you use to describe her?"

The middle-schooler stands for a moment. Then she clears her throat. "Loyal. Generous. Hard-working."

"Very nice. You can hand me your written portion and take your seat. Thank you, D'Brashia."

She nods and obeys, taking a seat. No one raises a hand to volunteer.

Miss Jettison scans the room. "Nevaeh. Come on up."

I take a cleansing breath. *Be with her, Lord. She's nervous about public speaking.*

Nevaeh walks to the back of the room and picks up a creation that appears made out of cardboard. As she walks past me, the cardboard, painted a brick color, resembles our church exterior. When I worked with her, the speech was about Heather, her friend and neighbor. What's the church about?

"I am thankful for…Mrs. Cheri." Her voice catches as she glances my way.

My chest tightens and my throat closes. *Don't cry, Cheri. Don't cry.*

Nevaeh focuses on her notes. "Most people know her from helping us here, and she's great at that. There's something about her smile that tells me everything's going to be okay. Mrs. Cheri also works at a church." She points at her cardboard work and lifts the top. "I couldn't get a ride, but I talked to Miss Wayson upstairs. Mrs. Cheri raised her, even though she's not a biological daughter. Miss Wayson explained that Mrs. Cheri helps her husband, the pastor. She also works with ladies and help them grow in their faith. But the upstairs of the church I made is where a group of ladies and teen girls meet once a month. Mrs. Cheri started that; it's called Linked."

Hot tears fall on my lap. I don't dare look anywhere but at my folded hands.

"I'm thankful for her because I know I'm not the only one she helps. Every day Mrs. Cheri pours herself into others. Not everyone is that nice. I know a lot of people think church people are fake, but not her. She's the real deal." Nevaeh offers an awkward bow and heads toward her seat.

We lock eyes and I mouth *thanks* as she takes her first steps.

Miss Jettison raises her index finger. "Please wait. Did you come up with this project on your own?"

Nevaeh nods. "I did. Why?"

The room temperature seems ten degrees colder. And dropping.

"I find it curious when this project started you said you were going to talk about Heather. Now, you're speaking about a staff member who worked one on one with you."

No, she did not just go there.

Nevaeh's eyes narrow and sparks are coming from them. Her jaw tightens and she stops next to her seat. "You think Mrs. Cheri forced me to talk about her?"

I want to stand, but I'm frozen in my seat, my legs shaking.

Miss Jettison scoffs. "It's quite a coincidence. And a convenient way for her to sneak her church talk into a school building."

Those words are the defrost I need to bolt from my chair. "Miss Jettison, I don't think now is the appropriate time to discuss this."

She glances my way as if I'm a mosquito she can't be bothered with, and returns her attention to Nevaeh, who has a vein in her forehead ready to pop. "Anyway, I have serious issues with your work. I'll look it over further and discuss it with your parents during conference."

Nevaeh shakes her head, her cheeks wet. "It's not fair. I'm thankful for her. I followed the directions."

Still, the woman isn't impressed and looks for the next student to present.

Lord, what do I do? I want to punch that woman. And hug Nevaeh.

The students offer nothing more than awkward coughs and stares toward Nevaeh. Pendleton is the next one to speak, and I try to keep composure and listen. Until I turn my head slightly and gasp.

Nevaeh's gone.

CHAPTER SEVENTEEN

Bethany

There's nothing like the dismissal bell starting a holiday break to clear the school halls. Even KJ ran past with a wave, happy to have a night off from basketball so she could go straight home. Me? The play is two weeks away. I'm on my way to practice.

When I get backstage, Darcy's already there with a bag of props open when I greet her. "Hey, Bethany. Glad you're here. I've been meaning to talk to you."

I stop and tilt my head, not sure what she's up to. Over the weeks I've gotten to know the team better, but I can't say Darcy and I are besties or anything. "What's up?"

"I didn't want to get in your business, especially with the others. I just wondered how you were doing after that video went school viral."

Oh, that. The night KJ spent the night and sobbed herself to sleep. "That's nice of you to ask. It was jarring when Brandon texted me and I watched it. His friends had fun with it, believing the worst about me and KJ. But, Mr. Burke also saw it, and that ended up being a blessing."

She looks up, a rubber chicken in hand. "How so?"

"The video, along with KJ and my documentation of things he's said and done, was proof of harassment. Although Sully claimed 'it could be anyone named Bethany and KJ,' Mr. Burke knew. We haven't pursued legal charges, but the jock's expelled. He sent us both a letter and promised not to bother us again."

Darcy rolls her eyes. "He'd better not."

I shrug. "Sully has to or he faces legal consequences. He apologized, and that closed the door for me."

Darcy throws a feather boa toward me. "What about KJ? Is she okay?"

I take it and wrap it around my neck, hot pink feathers tickle my cheek. "She will be. Her parents found a counselor. Sully really messed with her head." I notice Mr. Walsh and Brandon heading toward us. "Honestly, his teasing got to me as well. But I know who I am, and have a great support system. It's been a wild semester."

We chuckle, and Brandon is the first to reach us. His guitar strap hangs off his shoulder, and I stare at the waves in his hair thanks to a recent trim.

"You didn't start without me, did you?" His voice sounds melodic, even when he's not singing.

Darcy notices she's still holding the chicken, and drops it in the prop box like a discarded toy. "We're still missing the guys and Mackenzie. How do you think you did on the math test?"

Mr. Walsh joins us, and Brandon shrugs. "I studied. I finished. And it was tough."

Our advisor places his briefcase behind the props and claps his hands. "Talking about your tests today? I had a lot of kids dragging out of my class today with sad faces."

Jeff and Craig jog up with more energy than the rest of us.

Darcy moves a piece of her cotton candy-colored hair out of her eye. "I'm just glad the quarterly tests are done. Let's get to work. I'm ready to be in vacation mode."

Brandon nods and moves the guitar so he can strum. "I second that."

With the sketches Miss Briggs approved, we're actually laughing at our work. Although parts of the performance are interactive with the audience, the prop sketch and the sentences thrown in a hat work well. It flows so well that I don't notice it's almost seven.

Mr. Walsh glances at his watch. "Oh, wow. I was hoping to spring you guys by six-thirty. Should I let you go, or do we let Brandon sing?"

A flood of butterflies enters my stomach and flies around. *Let him sing. I'll even listen to two songs.*

Craig checks his phone. "I'm not in a hurry. Guys?" He glances around.

Jeff agrees. "Go for it, Brandon."

I also look at my phone, remembering my parents want a head's up text when rehearsal is almost over. Before Brandon postures himself and finds the right chord, a text comes through from mom.

"Hey Bethy, Dad and I are out to dinner in Columbiana. Sabrina's going to pick you up."

My parents on a date. Weird. Sabrina taking me home? Cool.

Brandon delivers a song based on Mr. Walsh's suggestion of eating too much turkey. By the last line, "Now I look like a turkey, too," we're overcome with laughter.

"Dude. You slayed that." Jeff stands and slaps Brandon's shoulder.

Darcy nods. "Seriously. You're better than the actual play." She looks to Mr. Walsh, whose eyes widen. "Don't tell Miss Briggs."

That brings more chuckles. Brandon waves us off. "You guys are too nice."

We start packing up, reaching for backpacks, taking care of props. My phone vibrates, and it's Sabrina letting me know she's outside.

I slide the phone in my pocket and place my backpack over my shoulder. "My ride is here. This is all going great. Thanks everyone for being a part of this. It means a lot." Who knew a stint in the principal's office would end up with a comedy troupe and new friends?

Brandon marches up, his hands stuffed in his pockets. "Hey. I'll walk out with you."

In the background I hear a "whoo-hoo" and giggles that I'm going to blame Darcy for. "Sounds great." My voice cracks, betraying me in my attempt to appear confident and not a freshman with Jell-O for knees.

We wave goodbye and take slow steps down the ramp toward the main halls. It wasn't that long ago we were leaving and Sully caught up. *Thank you, God, that I don't have to deal with him anymore.*

"So, KJ tells me your nickname is Bethy. Is that true?" He glances my way, revealing adorable dimples.

"Yep. One of those childhood mispronunciations."

He nods, hands still in pockets. "I like it. Can I call you that?"

I'm going to faint. I'm going to pass out in this hall and Sabrina will have to scoop me up and deliver me to my parents. "Absolutely."

"Good. Do you, um, go to Mugs?"

How have I not seen him there? "I practically live there."

He pushes on the front doors, gesturing for me to go first. "Maybe we could meet there over break."

I grab on the railing so I don't fall down the steps. "That would be great."

Sabrina honks her horn, and I lift my hand so she knows I see, and hopefully she'll stop honking already.

Brandon winks as our jackets touch. "Well, have a great weekend. I'll text you. Bethy." His voice is velvety and beautiful, and I basically float to Sabrina as he keeps walking to the student parking lot where his car is parked.

Sabrina doesn't even let me get in the car before she squeals. "Who is that? He is so cute. You need to spill."

I buckle in and sigh, taking a moment to drink the last ten minutes in.

Before I have the chance to speak, Sabrina digs in her purse. "I'm late getting this to you. Sorry. Things were stressful a few weeks ago, but it's all good." She hands me a white envelope with a golden seal on the back. My name is written in calligraphy.

"Is this your wedding invitation?"

Another squeal. "Charlie and I want to use everyone from Linked. Would you pass out programs?"

I carefully open the envelope. "Of course. I'd love to." I slide the beige invitation out, again in beautiful calligraphy. Saturday evening, December 8. "Wait. Am I reading this right?"

Her voice fills with dread. "What?"

"December 8?"

She nods. "Yes. Tell me you can come."

I close my eyes as I clutch the card stock. "It's one of the nights I have the play."

You're Brilliant

CHAPTER EIGHTEEN

Cheri

My announcement to Miss Jettison with a firm tone and steely gaze appears to communicate volumes.

She stops Pendleton's presentation and quickly makes her way to me. "What do you mean Nevaeh is gone?"

I try not to hiss my reply. "She is not in her chair. She's not in the restroom."

Miss Jettison's cheeks drain of color and she holds on to an empty desk for balance. "What have I done?"

Out of instinct I place a hand on her arm. "I'll go look for her."

She shakes her head. "No. Thank you. Watch the students. Have them read tonight's assignment. I'll leave. This is on me."

I nod. "Anything else?"

Her voice is nearly a whisper. "Please pray."

Once she leaves, I offer a fast, silent prayer before I turn and face the students. When I do, they are quiet and staring at me.

"Is Miss Jettison okay? She looked ready to cry."

I stride toward the front, hoping the questions are few. "Everything will be fine. If you read this now, you won't have homework tonight."

Pendleton raises his hand. "Where's Nevaeh?"

Gulp. *I'm not equipped, Lord.* "Miss Jettison is on her way to talk to her." I reach for the poetry book the students have been reading through. "Let's turn to page twenty-seven."

You're Brilliant

The bell rings and the kids shuffle to the hall. I bypass them all and head toward the office. Sheila's at the front window on the computer when I approach, out of breath. "Hi, Sheila. Have you seen Ellen?"

She keeps typing, but tilts her head toward the cafeteria.

The sixth graders are in line when I enter. In the opposite corner where three rows of bleachers rest, Miss Jettison is on the bottom row, sitting backwards, facing Nevaeh, who is just above. I can't tell what they're saying, but I see smiles. *Thank You, Jesus.* Not sure what to do, I return to the empty classroom and pray.

Ten minutes later, footsteps approach and I open my eyes. "Ellen. Is everything okay?"

Her eyes are bloodshot and face blotchy, and she's holding a tissue. "There's about fifteen minutes before next class. Do you mind if we talk?"

My heartbeat accelerates to the point that I think I can hear it in my ears. "Absolutely." I pull out Murina's chair and place it across from mine. "What happened?"

She dabs at her eyes with the tissue, taking the seat. "I've been teaching for fifteen years. I'm single, not dating. When I'm not here, I'm usually at my sister's house. She has two kids that I'm very close to." Her voice catches. "Last year my niece, Courtney, was diagnosed with lymphoma. What that poor girl has gone through."

"I had no idea. I'm so sorry. How is she doing?"

There's a small smile. "Court finished chemo and has a scan coming up. I've been working with her on schoolwork. She's in seventh grade. Very smart girl."

I smooth out the wrinkles in my skirt, not sure if I should say something or wait on her to continue.

Like a storm brewing, her disposition transitions, and her mood darkens. "I'm not proud of this, but since Courtney's diagnosis, I've been angry. I didn't realize how much so until Nevaeh ran off. My job is to be her cheerleader, not her bully." She dabs her eyes again. "It's the same with how I've treated you. Knowing you're a pastor's wife, I projected my anger at God toward you, spewing it everywhere with everyone without realizing how deep it was. Please forgive me."

I jump out of my chair and wrap my arms around her shoulders. "Of course. How can I help?" We both stand. She's still grasping the tissue like a life-line, but at least her smile is back.

"Forgiving me is everything. Nevaeh did the same. I plan on letting Mr. Tucker know what happened today. I'm prepared to talk with her family. Hopefully the consequences won't be severe. It would mean a lot to have a second chance to show everyone how much I enjoy teaching."

Ellen's eyes flash a glint of joy and hope for healing. I believe her.

"If you need me to watch a class or say something to Mr. Tucker, I'm happy to."

She reaches out with her free hand and squeezes mine. "Thank you, Cheri. I don't deserve your kindness. Maybe we could go out for coffee or something and get to know each other better."

I return the squeeze. "I'd love that."

You're Brilliant

After church, Sabrina and Charlie invite us to lunch, both full of giggles and enough energy to power a small city.

As Chet and I drive to meet them at Belleria's, he looks over with a grin. "Remember us at that age?"

The image of my poufy permed curls and leg warmers come instantly to mind. "You're as handsome now as then. I hope they are as blessed."

He nods. "Charlie's a solid man in Christ. They've had their bumps, and worked through it. I can't believe the wedding is a little over two weeks away. How hard do you think we'll cry?"

"Make sure you have a bucket on hand to capture my tears."

The lovebirds threaten my emotions once we settle in at the Italian eatery. Like Chet, Charlie holds the chair and doesn't sit until Sabrina and I are seated. They decide on their meals and place the menus aside, reaching to hold hands.

Chet loosens his tie. "How are the plans coming? You have everything happening around the same time."

The two exchange a gaze before looking at Chet. Charlie takes off his glasses and cleans them with the tail of his button-down shirt. "Everything with graduating and my new job is coming along. Packing is kind of chaotic, but I'm getting there. It's hard to know what clothes I need and what to pack."

Sabrina turns toward me. "There's a small glitch with the wedding, but we're praying about a solution that works for everyone."

She seems calm, so it must be the flowers, dresses, tuxes, and food are okay. "What's going on?"

"Bethany. We thought of things each of the Linked girls could do to be part of our day. We hoped Bethy could pass out programs. I picked her up after her comedy rehearsal the other night and she realized one of the play performances is the night of the wedding."

Oh, poor Bethy. "She must be disappointed."

Sabrina nods as the waitress places a basket of breadsticks between us. "She thinks it's her fault. It took quite a while once we got to her house for her to calm down. Between school starting, her friend KJ struggling thanks to that ex, and the comedy troupe, my save-the-date never really registered. When I handed her the invitation, it crushed her."

Charlie let go of her hand and reaches for a breadstick. "We hope she can be there. It's the last time Sabrina's going to see the girls before we move."

A sharp pang slices my stomach. I can't imagine Linked without Sabrina. "Oh, dear. We'll pray as well. Those girls love you so much."

Sabrina nibbles at the bottom of her lip for a moment. "Saying goodbye to all of you is going to be the hardest thing I've had to do as an adult. We're praying that once we settle and find a home church, maybe I can join or start a ministry similar to Linked."

"That, sweet girl, would be amazing."

We feast on breadsticks before Sabrina asks how things are going with Ellen Jettison.

"It's an answer to prayer. Once Ellen confided about her niece and how angry she was at God about it, it's like an invisible wall disappeared. We've had good chats."

"Is this teacher working on her feelings?" Charlie asks.

"I think so. She's certainly improved in the classroom. Laughing, encouraging the kids. Everything you want to see in a teacher."

Chet smiles. "I'm so proud of you, Cheri. When you started working at the school, I knew you were nervous. You found your niche there and God is using you. It sounds like Ellen trusts you."

"It's true. I was in line at the copy machine and when she noticed me, she asked if I was the niece you raised. When I confirmed it, Ellen got all misty and said she hopes her influence on Courtney will be as amazing as what you've done for me." Sabrina sips her ice water.

Wow. To God be the glory. There's no way I could take credit for that turnaround.

"Honey, I have a question. Have you invited this woman to church?"

CHAPTER NINETEEN

Bethany

It's a drizzling Saturday morning that calls for hot chocolate. Hayley, Jazmin and I are at Mugs with Lena and Mrs. Cheri.

"What time is Sabrina arriving?" Lena nurses a peppermint leaf tea while I play with the whipped cream on top of my drink.

Mrs. Cheri adds milk to her coffee. "Ten minutes. She should be surprised. I left the house before she came downstairs."

Jazmin pulls a bright pink envelope out of her backpack. "I can't believe this is our last Linked outing with her."

I should've ordered the peppermint tea to calm my stomach. "How do you think I feel? I'm missing the wedding. I'm so stupid. I can't believe I didn't remember the date was the same as the play." Fresh tears threaten.

Mrs. Cheri's the first to reach over with her hand on my arm. "Now Bethy, there's no negative talk allowed. You've had a lot on your mind. It's an honest mistake."

Lena smiles. "We're also thinking of ways to get you there and not miss the play."

I look around the table. They're my cheerleaders. I'd be lost without them.

Sabrina enters Mugs shaking her red umbrella and looking for Lena, who sent her a text. We're in the corner with balloons tied to the chair we have ready for our bride-to-be. She notices and a cry escapes. "You guys! I can't believe this."

Lena giggles. "We can't let you get married without a Linked shower."

We each stand and give her a hug before she takes her seat.

You're Brilliant

"And a caffeinated one at that." Hayley hands Sabrina a hot mocha with caramel.

"The best kind." Sabrina raises her mug. "To Linked."

I hoist my red stoneware in the air. "To Sabrina and Charlie."

We enjoy our drinks and catch up on wedding plans. The pit in my stomach continues to grow.

Sabrina looks over and tilts her head. "Hey. You aren't beating yourself up about the play, are you?"

Jazmin nudges my arm. "Only all week."

Mrs. Cheri reaches for her phone. "Girls, let's figure this out. There has to be a way Bethany can be a part of the wedding and the play."

Both are in the evening. In different suburbs.

"The wedding is at six. Bethy, what time does the opening skit begin?"

Mr. Walsh's instructions come to mind. *Curtains open at seven. First skit starts twenty seconds after that.* "I'm supposed to be there at six-fifteen. We go on at seven. I'm not in the first skit, but the second. And then I introduce the actual play."

There's a few moments of silence, minus the sips of drink.

Lena's the first to speak. "Your job is handing out the programs. That's from five-thirty to six. Can you move out the time you have to be at school? After all, you aren't in the first skit."

I picture myself in a dress and heels changing clothes in a church bathroom. "I can ask Mr. Walsh."

Sabrina taps the table. "It's possible you could be at the church until six, change, and have your parents drive you to school. It could put you there before seven. Even if it's late, I see no reason why you can't be there by five after."

Hayley sighs. "It's tight, but doable."

Jazmin raises her eyebrows. "If her drama teacher agrees."

"Then once the skits are over, you could come back. Or, watch the play and you'd definitely be there for most of the reception." Sabrina's smile gives me hope.

Hayley can't help but giggle. "And bring Brandon with you for a slow dance."

I roll my eyes as I pull out my phone. "I'll text Mr. Walsh and explain the conflict. He should understand."

Mrs. Cheri folds her hands. "I'm going to say a little prayer that he does."

Ten minutes later, with Mr. Walsh's help, we have a plan that puts me at the church to hand out programs and watch Sabrina walk down the aisle, yet has me at the school for the skit. My parents are in charge of when I leave the play and arrive at the reception.

"Thank you. I felt defeated all week. I wanted to do both but didn't see how. I appreciate all of you."

Sabrina's lip trembles for a few seconds. "I'm going to miss you all."

Lena pulls her phone out of her purse. "Then we need to get a group picture so we can frame it for you." She stands, and I notice a little bump under her sweater.

Jazmin gasps, but doesn't say anything.

Lena looks over and laughs. "Oh, right. I told the ladies, but forgot about you girls. I'm expecting."

Hayley squeals. "Another family to babysit!"

Brandon's curls bounce as he finds his way backstage. "A family just stopped me to say my song was the highlight of the night."

Mackenzie lets out a squeal. "I heard a couple talking. They said the comedy troupe should be a main feature and not an opening act."

Mr. Walsh joins us. "Excellent first performance. You hit your marks. The audience loved you all."

Darcy closes her eyes for a moment, then lets out a deep breath. "I've never been so nervous."

KJ arrives, holding a bouquet of burnt orange mums and yellow snapdragons. "The show was amazing. You all rocked it." She hands me the flowers, still in the cellophane wrapping. "Bethy, everyone laughed so hard when you grabbed that hula-hoop out of the prop box."

I hug her and smell the autumn flowers. "Thank you. I agree with Darcy. I was so scared. There were more people in the audience than I thought there would be."

Everyone nods.

Mr. Walsh chuckles. "That's what tonight is about. Get the nerves out. Work any kinks out. And come back tomorrow and do it all over again."

I glance around and observe the same look on my friends that matches how I feel. "Mr. Walsh, my nerves aren't completely out yet."

You're Brilliant

CHAPTER TWENTY

CHERI

When Sabrina descends the stairs the morning of the wedding, Chet's hand steadies my back as I sniffle. "Sweetheart, she isn't even in her dress yet."

Sabrina gaze locks with mine, her kind blue eyes that always seem as big as her heart, pooling with tears. "Mom. How are we going to make it through the ceremony?"

Chet welcomes our precious child into a family embrace. "Oh, there's no way we're going to. But that's okay. All the tears today are happy ones."

Her wedding day moves as fast as mine did. Even with an evening ceremony, we have a brunch with Sabrina's father, my brother-in-law, who I'm proud to say is at the eighteen-month sobriety mark.

"Sorry I wasn't much of a father." He clears his throat as he looks at Chet. "You ended up in great hands though, Sabrina."

She extends her hands and reaches for both men to give each of their hands a squeeze. "I have the best in both of you."

After brunch, the bridal party arrives at the hair salon. Sabrina goes first. When she emerges forty-five minutes later, our little girl looks like a princess. Her blonde locks are pinned with spiral curls cascading down. A silver tiara rests on top of her head.

Lena, in a chair with a towel draped over her, covers her mouth and starts to move.

The stylist holds the straightener in her hand. "I need you to sit still. You could get burned."

Lena nods, then catches herself moving. "Sorry." She gazes straight ahead. "Sabrina, I knew you were beautiful, but today you're extra stunning."

Sabrina waves her off. "Stop. I'm wearing sweatpants with grape jelly on them."

Once we reach the church, we trade our casual attire for dresses. The photographer chuckles as Sabrina lifts her dress to her ankles to reveal tennis shoes matching the turquoise bridesmaids' dresses.

Hayley twirls in her floor length dress. "I could wear this every day."

Jazmin turns from the full-length mirror and faces her friend from school. "The dress matches your eyes. You're gorgeous."

I clasp the pearl necklace my mother gave me on my wedding day. "All of you are absolutely beautiful. What a day God has given us."

The walk down the aisle is hard to take in. Our church family takes up most of the pews. Sabrina's fellow teachers. Charlie's students and other doctoral candidates. Neighbors. Miss Jettison smiles as I pass her. *Lord, You are so good. Thank You for all You've done in her life.*

Once seated, Charlie breaks from the men and walks over to me with a corsage matching the blue and pink bridal flowers. He puts it on and kisses my cheek. "I promise I'll take great care of her."

He's back with Chet and his groomsmen before I find my voice to thank him.

My tissue is wrinkled in the palm of my hand when the bridal march begins. We stand, and my gasp joins the chorus of others. I can see the sparkles from the back of the sanctuary. The glorious white of her dress. But none of it compares to her smile. For all the tears she shed as a little girl trying to process rejection and her parent's addiction, her life is full.

As she passes my pew, Rod, looking dapper in his tux as he holds her arm to his chest, gazes straight ahead. Sabrina does as well, her head held high with her deliberate steps toward Charlie.

The groom's hands shake as Rod proclaims he's the one giving her away, and Chet nods. Charlie takes Sabrina's hands and her dad returns to his seat.

Sabrina leans in. "Hey. Thanks for showing up."

Charlie laughs, and even Chet chuckles.

The ceremony continues, the perfect balance of love, humor, and covenant thinking. When Chet announces the couple as man and wife, I reach for my third tissue.

"Ladies and gentlemen, I present to you Mr. and Mrs. Charlie Shell."

The couple hold hands and glide to the back of the church to greet everyone. When Chet and I reach them, Sabrina wraps her arms around my neck. "I love you, Mom."

"Baby girl, I love you, too. You're the most beautiful bride."

She releases her grip. "I'm going to need help buttoning up my train before I leave."

"No worries. Lena and I will help."

Charlie and Sabrina chose the Mill Creek Park reception center for their twilight party. With a dome skylight showcasing the moonlit evening, it's as if God has helped decorate. Mums line the sidewalk as Chet and I walk to the glass doors awaiting our cue to enter.

"Save a dance for me?" Chet's whisper is as romantic as the night.

"Absolutely."

Behind us, Lena's sweet giggle fills the air as she enjoys an evening with Bryce.

"It's been a perfect wedding." I sigh, hearing the DJ greeting the pumped-up crowd.

Chet nods. "I think he's ready to announce us."

An hour later, I enjoy a few bites of pork loin and sautéed apple slices before pushing my plate back. "Have you ever been too happy to eat?"

Chet pats his middle-age stomach. "That's not something I can relate to."

Jazmin raises her hand. "Does anyone have extra bread? I'm still hungry."

The DJ starts his fast tempo playlist when Bethany and her parents arrive. She's still in her skit outfit when Sabrina greets her with a long hug. The rest of the Linked team follows.

"How was the play?" Hayley asks.

Bethany's eyes sparkle. "It was a full house. Everyone laughed. But I'm so glad I could be here."

Sabrina steps back, realizing Charlie is at her side. "We are too. Don't forget to visit the cookie table. Charlie's grandma worked all week on them."

Jazmin's eyes widen. "God bless the Youngstown cookie table at weddings. See ya." She heads toward the room full of tables and cookies.

Bethany looks to her parents. "Now that the play is done, I'm hungry. I've been too nervous to eat."

Charlie points to a table up front. "The wait staff kept your meals warm. Enjoy."

Hayley glances at Lena. "We should probably visit the cookie table before Jazmin clears it out."

Sabrina giggles. "She's right. You better get in there."

The exodus in search of cookies leaves Chet, Charlie, Sabrina, and me. The newlyweds hold hands and never stop smiling.

"You have slow songs planned, right?" I ask, winking at my husband.

Charlie smiles. "Absolutely."

Almost on cue, the tempo slows, and the lights dim. Charlie nudges Sabrina. "Time to dance."

She waves and makes her way to the dance floor.

Chet reaches for my hand. "I can't believe it."

We stroll to the dance area and start to sway. "What?"

"We're empty nesters."

I wait for the grief, but it doesn't hit just yet. Looking around there's victories and opportunities as we pass Charlie and Sabrina. Bryce and Lena. Glancing at the front table, I find Bethany finishing her meal as Jazmin and Hayley join her with cookies in their hands. "True. But we have something else."

You're Brilliant

Chet's breath dances past my ear. "What's that?"

"Full hearts."

THE END

IF YOU LOVED YOU'RE BRILLIANT:

It would mean a lot if you would leave a review on Amazon, BookBub, and Goodreads. The more reviews a book has, the more publicity it receives on Amazon.

A review can be as short as "I really liked it!" If you aren't sure what to write, you can share a couple things that stood out to you, as long as you don't give the plot away. If you know us "in real life," don't mention that. Thank you for taking the time to share your thoughts and to help us get this important message out to girls of all ages.

A Note from the Authors:

If you have ever experienced anything close to what KJ did with Sully, please know that is abuse and unacceptable. For fiction reasons we allowed KJ and Sully to date. However, if they were real, we would never encourage someone to date to achieve popularity, especially if the other person is a bully.

If anything close to KJ's story rings true for you, please tell a trusted adult. It can be a parent, a teacher, principal, or a pastor's wife.

The true defeated one, the devil, has limited resources and will use whatever bag of tricks he can that will work. He loves to lie and make us feel like we are dumb, because the truth is, he's defeated. We were created as God's masterpiece, the piece de resistance. We are brilliant. YOU are brilliant. That is the truth. Receive and live it out, and please let others know about this book. We truly want to change lives with our words, and one of the most important messages a girl can hear is she's brilliant!

Acknowledgements:

Hannah:

Mrs. Gordon, Ms. Yargo, Ms. Shanice, and Ms. Lori, thank you for encouraging me and believing in me. For asking about this book and how I am doing.

For Mr. Duane and Mrs. Tracie and everyone involved in respite nights and Night to Shine for making me feel extra beautiful.

Pastor Matt, Lizz, Miss Deb, Miss Heidi, Miss Shannon, Miss Shelly, Miss Susie, Annie, and Mr. Dan, I appreciate you having my back at youth group.

Amilia, Kayla, Kaylee, and Katie your friendship and encouragement mean so much to me. I love you guys.

For Mrs. Rhonda, for helping us come up with the name of the series just by being Southern.

Randy, Mandy, Oliver, Matt, Stephanie, James, and Grace, I love my Wisconsin family.

Grandma, Aunt Crista, and Landon. You always cheer me on. Thank you!

Brian, you're a great brother, even if I pretend to be annoyed by you. Brianna, thanks for keeping Brian in line!

Dad, thanks for everything you do for our family and how you make me smile. And for lunch money.

Mom, thanks for taking me out of my comfort zone by hearing my story idea and making it real. For believing in me.

Jesus, You told my parents before I was born that I would be an overcomer. Thank You for being a keeper of promises.

Julie:

Hannah, you challenge and inspire me daily to keep shining bright for Christ even when times are tough. In a difficult season, you chose better over bitter. More than that, you came up with a series that I believe was God sent to encourage many. You are amazing.

Scribes 202, this book wasn't a normal submission given my contemporary romance background, but you dove in without reservation or hesitation. Thank you for all your help. I couldn't write without you.

Shirley, Ruth, Kara, Deb, Tracie, Summer, Brenda, Rita, Noreen, and Amy. Your prayers literally cover everything in my life. Thank you for keeping this project and our family in prayer.

Tami, thank you for reminding me how KJ's story needed to be told and hearts like hers be encouraged.

Sermon Central for the outline to the fox and the henhouse sermon.

To the real "Linked" ministry, the story and conflict are fiction, but the love, prayers, and friendships between the ages were definitely borne out of everything we experienced in this real ministry.

Pastor Gary and Rhonda Gray for allowing me to share sermon notes, and for Rhonda inspiring the name of the series and being all around wonderful.

Randy, Mandy, Oliver, Matt, Stephanie, James, and Grace, thank you for loving Hannah, Brian, and me from the first moment we entered your lives.

Brian, you had your own refiner's fire at the same time Hannah was trusting God through hers. The pure gold that is showing itself from that season blesses and teaches me. Keep believing Him, even and especially when the world disappoints. Brianna, you're an answer to prayer and an amazing prayer warrior. Keep Believing God.

Tom, thanks for being among the first to show me true freedom comes when I surrender negative thinking. I've grown because you taught me to give people the benefit of the doubt, and reminded me that God promised to lead us through the fire, not around it. Thanks for asking.

Jesus, I didn't see any of this coming, the adversity or the series. You did, and I appreciate the grace as I processed the hurt, grief, lament, and the beginning of healing. Not a word, not a breath is possible without You. It is all for the furthering of Your Kingdom and Your glory.

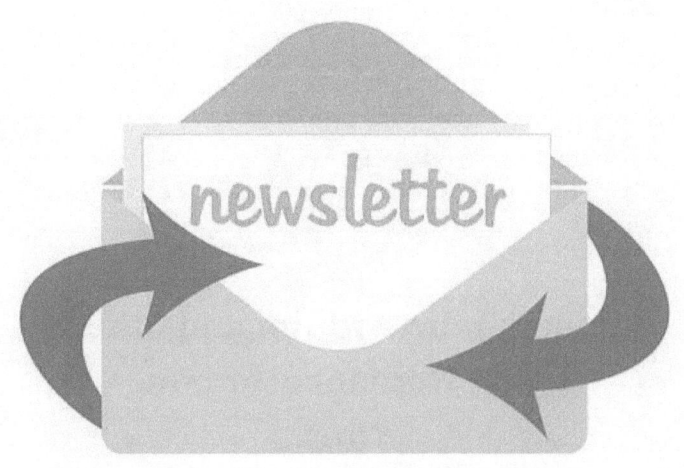

**The Julie Arduini Newsletter
delivers to your email twice a month.**
Per reader request, one time is a writing update and book suggestions.

The second time is a brief encouragement and any news that benefits you.

To thank new subscribers, you receive Book 1, *Entrusted* and Book 2, *Entangled*, in the Surrendering Time Series.

To subscribe for free, visit http://juliearduini.com and click on the right sidebar.

Fall in Love with a Good Book

Follow Julie Arduini and other Inspy Romance authors:

Blog:

http://inspyromance.com

Twitter:

http://twitter.com/inspyromance

Facebook:

http://facebook.com/inspyromance

Pinterest:

http://pinterest.com/inspyromance

CHRISTIANS READ

Follow Julie Arduini and other Christian authors at Christians Read.
Blog:
http://christiansread.wordpress.com
Facebook:
http://facebook.com/christiansread
Twitter:
http://twitter.com/christiansread

Looking for
an Encouraging Speaker?

Julie Arduini is passionate about encouraging audiences to find freedom through surrender. She's able to speak on a wide range of surrender topics, the writing process, family, motherhood, and her own books.

Learn more by contacting her at

juliearduini@juliearduini.com

.

Regan's Acts of Kindness

Although I never met Regan, her parents spent a lot of time with our family when we lived in Upstate NY. Regan was taken from them in January 2017. She would have turned five in March.

Everyone who loved Regan wants her to be remembered. Here are different ways you can help make that happen: **Like Regan's Acts of Kindness on Facebook and participate.** http://facebook.com/RegansActsofKindness **Paint Rocks and Hide them in appropriate places in your community.** Check the Facebook page above to learn how to tag them to keep the kindness flowing. **Visit Regan's Corner at The Wild Animal Park in Chittenango, New York** http://thewildpark.com

Other Books by Julie Arduini

Contemporary Romance
The Surrendering Time Series:
Entrusted:
https://www.amazon.com/gp/product/B01FGC1Z8W
Entangled:
https://www.amazon.com/gp/product/B01FG7JALG
Engaged
https://www.amazon.com/gp/product/B072K91W25
Finding Freedom Through Surrender: 30-Day Devotional featuring characters and themes from the Surrendering Time series:
https://www.amazon.com/gp/product/B06XBHM2P3

Surrendering Opinions
Anchored: Coming Winter 2020

Stand-Alone Christian Romance
Match Made in Heaven
https://www.amazon.com/Match-Made-Heaven-Julie-Arduini-ebook/dp/B07QR29X51/

Restoring Christmas
https://www.amazon.com/Restoring-Christmas-Novella-Julie-Arduini-ebook/dp/B07ZDHX954

Surrendering Stinkin' Thinkin' Series with Hannah Arduini:
You're Beautiful:
https://www.amazon.com/gp/product/B078VK3JJB
You're Amazing
https://www.amazon.com/Youre-Amazing-Surrendering-Stinkin-Thinkin-ebook/dp/B07M7D6HSV
You're Brilliant

https://www.amazon.com/Youre-Brilliant-Surrendering-Stinkin-Thinkin-ebook/dp/B0874Y5B4C

A Walk in the Valley Infertility Devotional Workbook with Heidi Glick, Elizabeth Maddrey, Kym McNabney, Paula Mowery and Donna Winters
https://www.amazon.com/Walk-Valley-Christian-encouragement-infertility-ebook/dp/B06XC36GMV

About the Authors:

Hannah Arduini is in the tenth grade and lives outside of Youngstown, Ohio. She loves fashion, Starbucks, and serving at church. She has a brother who lives at home, and siblings who live in Wisconsin. She also has two nephews and a niece. *You're Beautiful*, *You're Amazing*, and *You're Brilliant* are products of her imagination.

Julie Arduini loves to encourage readers to find freedom in Christ by surrendering the good, the bad, and ---maybe one day---the chocolate. She's the author of the contemporary romance series SURRENDERING TIME, (Entrusted, Entangled, Engaged,) as well as the stand-alone novellas, MATCH MADE IN HEAVEN and RESTORING CHRISTMAS. She also shares her story in the infertility devotional, A WALK IN THE VALLEY. Her other latest release, YOU'RE BRILLIANT, is for girls ages 10-100, written with her teenaged daughter, Hannah, and is book 3 in their SURRENDERING STINKIN' THINKIN' series. She blogs every other Wednesday for Christians Read, as well as monthly with Inspy Romance. She resides in Ohio with her husband and two children. Learn more by visiting her at http://juliearduini.com, where she invites readers to opt in to her content full of resources and giveaway opportunities.

Facebook: http://facebook.com/JulieArduini

Twitter: http://twitter.com/JulieArduini

Pinterest: http://pinterest.com/JulieArduini

Instagram: http://instagram.com/JulieArduini

Snapchat: https://www.snapchat.com/add/JulieArduini

Goodreads: http://goodreads.com/JulieArduini

Amazon:http://www.amazon.com/Julie-Arduini/e/B00PBKDRSQ/

BookBub: https://www.bookbub.com/profile/julie-arduini

Newsletter:https://mailchi.mp/321e32f02e17/juliearduininewsletter

www.ingramcontent.com/pod-product-compliance
Lightning Source LLC
Chambersburg PA
CBHW022023170626
46808CB00003B/1043